SNARE IN THE BLIND ALLEY

A VIKING WITCH MYSTERY

CATE MARTIN

Cover design by Shezaad Sudar.

Rune art by BettyStrange at Dreamstime.com.

Ratatoskr Press logo by Aidan Vincent Kise.

ISBN 978-1-965167-49-6

❈ Formatted with Vellum

CHAPTER ONE

Every fall, tourists from all over the Midwest and beyond flock to the towns on the North Shore of Lake Superior, desperate to soak up the truly spectacular colors of the changing leaves. They flock to all the hiking trails, to the ski lifts that take them up to the hilltops for the full panoramic experience, and to the entire length of the Gunflint Trail as it winds through the forest teaming with wildlife from the shore of Lake Superior all the way to the Boundary Waters.

But all of that really happens from mid-September to early October. Driving in my little Volkswagen now, two days before Halloween, all of those tourists had followed the peak colors to the south. Which made the drive a lot more relaxing, and even past their peak, the trees were still bringing a fine mix of bright colors this year.

Or rather, the lack of traffic on the highway and the beauty of the natural world around us *should* have made the drive more relaxing. But the truth was, I could feel a great deal of nervousness emanating from the passengers in my car. And I was contributing to it myself.

I glanced into the rearview mirror, just long enough to see that my friend Kara Mikkelsen was still chewing at her lip as she gazed out the window at the passing scenery. At least her hands had stopped twisting together in anxiety. But that was only because her husband,

Thorge Valkisson, had taken one of her hands in his to stop their motion. Now she just clutched at his hand with both of hers, so tightly her knuckles had gone white.

Not that I could blame her for being nervous. She—as well as Thorge and his brother Thorbjorn, who sat in the front beside me— had grown up in a hidden village, tucked away from the rest of the world by powerful magic. The village had been originally settled centuries before by Vikings who had found themselves quite suddenly very far from home with no way back.

Which isn't to say that it exists in the past. Time has passed there the same as it has in the rest of the world. It's no less modern than where I had grown up in St. Paul, Minnesota.

But time has passed differently there. Such a small community had very little need for cars, for instance. The people of Villmark knew of the existence of cars, and quite a few of the younger generations had spent time in one or two on occasion. So our drive today wasn't in and of itself what was making them nervous.

No, it wasn't the modern technology that had everyone else in my admittedly decades-old Volkswagen on edge.

It wasn't even the fact that this drive today was removing Kara and Thorge from the only home they'd ever known, to thrust them alone into a strange world far from the support of their families, where they would have to stay for at least the next four months.

No, what had us all so nervous that day was the reason for that separation: Kara's high-risk pregnancy.

Not that anything seemed wrong with her so far. She was five months along, just barely showing the first signs of a baby bump on her muscular frame.

She looked like a valkyrie. She looked like the sturdy sort of woman who would find herself going into labor out in the farm fields and birth the baby on her own, then promptly get back to the work of her farm. Maybe you know the type. Or you've seen one in a movie.

But we all had good reason to fear that might not actually be the case with Kara. Because, despite the hardy look of all the women in her family, there was a long history of difficult pregnancies, most of which had ended tragically.

There were a couple of midwives back in Villmark, as well as a few doulas, all with years of experience with pregnancy, delivery, and babies in general. Kara had been tended to by all of them over the last couple of months, and none of them felt like there was any reason for alarm yet.

Yet. They never forgot to add that word. Yet.

Luckily for Kara and Thorge, though, we had options. For one, Thorge's father Valki was one of the council of three who governed the people of Villmark. So the usual rule about not allowing Vill-markers who went out into the greater world to return was suspended without any pushback from the other two on the council.

Secondly, I happened to have two close friends who lived in Duluth. Jesús Rodríguez I had known from my days working as a server in a restaurant in St. Paul. He had come north when his sister Tlalli had started nursing school here, and our paths had crossed again quite coincidentally. Jesús had always been a good friend to me, and when I had asked for help finding an apartment close to any of the best hospitals and clinics of Duluth, he had gladly stepped up.

Now, if anything did go wrong with Kara's pregnancy, she would be in a much better position to deal with it, living in Duluth.

But the best part of all was Tlalli. Because, not only was she going to school to be a nurse and already had a ton of skills under her belt, she was also something else. Something more.

She, like me and my grandmother before me, could work magic. It wasn't quite the same magic as I did. What my grandmother and I practiced had been passed down in a direct line from the days of our ancestor Torfa, the woman who had brought her people to the shores of Lake Superior centuries ago by magical means and had set up the protections that kept them all safe from harm. We were volvas, and our magic was thoroughly Viking.

But Tlalli's magic came from her childhood in Mexico City, bits learned from her mother and grandmother that she only remembered in fragments. Since then, she had been learning more from a Celtic woman that my grandmother had hooked her up with in Duluth.

Her traditions might be thoroughly different from mine, but her raw power was probably greater than mine. At least, I'd thought so the few times I had seen her wield it. At any rate, I felt so much better at the thought of leaving Kara and Thorge alone in a strange city that didn't function anything like what they were used to knowing that Tlalli would be there, looking out for them in any way they needed it.

Beside me, Thorbjorn shifted slightly, trying to catch a glimpse of the map on my cellphone that was attached to a mount that was angled more to face me than him. It was a small movement, but impossible to miss. Being well over six feet tall, and what I'm sure only felt like as wide across his massive shoulders, he took up two-thirds of the front seat of my little Volkswagen.

Not that he jostled me at all, not even the hand I kept resting on the stick shift even though I hadn't changed gears in miles.

Not that I would've objected if he had.

He had been gone in the north for months, and I hadn't known for all that time when I'd see him again, if ever. Having him back with me was still a new experience even after five weeks, one I was still relishing all over again whenever I was freshly aware of his presence.

Like now. He wasn't touching me, but I could feel the warmth of him. I could smell that foresty smell of him, stronger even than the always faintly burnt smell that came out of my old car's heat vents.

"We're nearly there," I told him, guessing why he'd wanted to look at my phone. He had spent the night before studying the map of where we were going thoroughly. Like a military leader of old, planning a sortie. While my cellphone worked in Villmark, and I could even charge it there using the modest power that ran through the town from the solar panels the council maintained, I didn't have a printer to make him a paper copy of our route. But I had sketched it out for him, and he had studied that sketch with great intensity. So I knew he knew that we were nearly there since we'd just passed a bunch of signs showing the way to get off the highway to see Gooseberry Falls.

"Yes," was all he said, scratching at his trim strawberry-blond beard.

I don't know how I knew, but I was sure I knew what he was thinking in that moment. Or, more specifically, who he was missing.

Our mutual friend Loke Grímsson. Few in Villmark spent as much time in the greater world as Loke had. He even had an alter ego in that larger world, going by the less question-provoking name of Luke.

He would've been the perfect addition to our little party. Not only was he comfortable everywhere he went, he also had a power I didn't quite understand the mechanics of: he could open a door anywhere in the world and step through it to emerge from some other door in some other place. He didn't always have perfect control for where he went on his own—something about how his magic worked tended to drag him away to where he felt like he was meant to do something no matter his own goals for opening the door in the first place—but with others, he had never failed to get to where he meant to go.

But if Loke had been with us, there wouldn't have been any need to take the car at all. He could just bring us straight to Talli and Jesús' apartment, and then after seeing what was going to be Kara and Thorge's place, he could bring us straight home again. And once he'd seen it, he could get back to it directly anytime he wanted to.

Alas, he wasn't with us. He wasn't even in Villmark. He had left one day months ago with Thorbjorn, heading to points unknown far to the north of Villmark. Thorbjorn had only recently returned, but Loke had yet to return at all.

I missed him. Not his power, useful as that could be, and not his capacity to deal with the greater world. I missed *him*. My friend.

My darkly sarcastic friend with the wide, mischievous grin.

He had gone north seeking answers to more questions than he had been willing to share with me, I knew. And this hadn't just been north in the conventional sense of the term. Because everything north of Runde, the Minnesotan town that had grown up around the borders of the hidden settlement of Villmark, was more of Minnesota and then all of Canada.

No, he had gone north of *Villmark*, north of the settlement Torfa had founded but still on that side of the veil of magic that hid it from the greater world.

The people of Villmark always referred to everything north of them as the road to Old Norway. And certainly the mountains that could be seen in the distance looked like the peaks of the mountains of Norway, all ice and rock and snow-swept summits.

But the further north you went, the more twisted space and time became. I didn't think it was possible to walk all the way to Norway, modern or old or any other version of it. And I didn't think that had been where Loke had been trying to go, anyway.

But he was lost now, somewhere between Villmark and Old Norway. And while we had gotten a few hints at where he might be and what he might be up to, they were only the vaguest of hints. Not even Thorbjorn—who had journeyed with him until Loke had sent him away to carry on alone—knew where to find him now.

He would come home on his own someday, I knew. But so far, no day had been that day. Although every morning when I got up I did what little magic I could to try to sense his presence. This morning, like all the others, he hadn't been near enough for me to feel.

But he would be back.

And in the meantime, I had people to care for. Very anxious people. I could only do my best to make them comfortable in their new, if temporary, home.

And try not to think about how, if they ever needed me, I would be a two-hour drive away. Try not to think about how much could go wrong in two hours.

CHAPTER TWO

THE MAP on my phone brought us straight to the apartment building easily enough. And on that perfect late October day, unseasonably warm but not excessively so, navigating the steep streets of Duluth wasn't a problem. And while parking on the street in my old Volkswagen with its manual transmission wasn't something I had done in the last year, muscle memory kicked in and I accomplished the task quite handily.

But I admit there was already a nervous gnawing in my belly. Snow would fly, and I doubted that was even so much as a month away from now. Snow and ice were going to make both of the two steep roads that flanked the apartment building suddenly treacherous. And it wasn't just the street parking I was worried about. It was the mere act of driving. My tires were in reasonably good shape, but still, my car was a far cry from a four-wheel-drive behemoth in snow tires.

If I started to skid, if I lost control on either of those roads, hitting another car or light post or something was actually the best-case scenario. Because worst case?

Well, both of those roads carried on straight down the steep hill, ending at the lake itself. And that water was already cold enough to kill, even on a day as warm as today.

"Ingrid?" Thorbjorn said, pulling me out of my thoughts. Kara and Thorge in the back seat were looking at me anxiously as well. It was like none of them wanted to move, not even to open one of the car doors, until I gave them the all clear.

"It's nothing," I said, and pulled the keys out of the ignition.

"You didn't… sense anything?" Kara asked.

"No, nothing's wrong," I said. "I'm just thinking, when I drive here in the future, I might have to park a little further away. Not on this hill. But not today. We're fine here now, and no one wants to haul those boxes further than we have to, right?"

"You're worried about ice," Thorbjorn said at last.

"Oh, of course," Kara said with palpable relief.

Then we all got out of the car, and I, for one, got my first good look at the building itself, not just its location on my phone navigation app. It was across the street from where I had parked, directly in Kara's line of sight on the passenger side of the car, and I could see why she was nervous I might have sensed something untoward about it.

I mean, it was an impressive structure, to be sure. The three-story brick building was more than a century old, but well-maintained and built to last. The cornices and other details were stone, and the brick only gave hints of its past in a much smoggier city before clean air laws and just the passage of time had made smoke obsolete.

It had once been a posh hotel, if not quite as posh as the Spaulding Hotel back when it had still been standing. But this hotel was a couple of blocks west of the heart of Duluth, halfway up the hillside, hence the steep streets.

But even from the street level, I could see that any window in that building above the second floor was going to have an impressive view of either the harbor and lake to the east, or of the ridgeline to the west. Which was looking particularly picturesque at the moment, with all the leaves in their lush fall colors, only a little faded.

I took out my phone and sent a quick text to Tlalli and Jesús, who were waiting in the apartment for our arrival. Then I tucked the phone in my back pocket and opened the hatch at the back of my car.

There were six boxes and an equal number of oversized gym bags in the trunk area. Everything that Kara and Thorge were bringing with them from home, mostly clothes but also some personal items. Which was why Tlalli and Jesús were upstairs already.

Because on top of finding us this rental in the first place, Tlalli had also gone all-out with thrifting to furnish the space. My grandmother had reimbursed her for every expense, but the cost to her in time, her with a full plate of nursing school on top of part-time work and continuing her magical training, was a true gift to Kara and Thorge. A couple she had met exactly twice, even if the second time had been at their wedding.

"Let's take the boxes first," I said. "We can come back down for the bags, but I'm going to lock the car in the meantime. The neighborhood looks fine, but better safe than sorry."

I felt like I was over-explaining, but random theft wasn't exactly an issue in Villmark, so maybe it really did need to be said out loud.

Thorbjorn and Thorge both just nodded, and after a brief bit of kerfuffle when Kara refused to put down the box she had picked up or to let Thorge take it from her, we all crossed the street and headed west, uphill, towards the front lobby entrance of the building.

A pair of figures was just coming down the stairs at the back of the lobby as we came in through the outer set of doors at the entrance. The inner doors were not only locked, but their glass was fogged with handprints, and the lobby interior beyond was too dark to see details. But the pair of figures approached the other side of the door, and one of them pushed the door open to let us in.

It was, of course, Tlalli and Jesús, holding the door to let us all troop inside.

Jesús was short and wiry with his dark brown hair pulled back into a short ponytail, his sister Tlalli a little taller and rounder with a much thicker and longer ponytail that sat higher on her head. But they shared the same crooked smile and sparkling warmth in their dark eyes.

Jesús whisked the box out of my arms so that Tlalli could pull me into a quick hug. Then that box was thrust back at me so they could do the same with Kara.

"How is it going?" Tlalli asked her, in her nurse voice that meant it wasn't just a gesture of politeness, that question.

"I was a little woozy in the car, but I'm better now," Kara told her. Which was certainly news to me. If I had known she was getting carsick, I might've done something about it.

Or *tried* to do something about it, even if there was little to be done. Which was probably why she hadn't mentioned it. Kara *hated* being fussed over.

"It's three floors up with no elevator, but that's how we got it at such a steal," Jesús warned us as he, still carrying Kara's box, led the way back up the stairs he had just come down. "Well, that and the fact that it's a bit—"

"Cozy," Tlalli finished for him.

The stairwell had once been a grand feature, I could tell, back in the hotel's heyday. Alas, the art déco carpet I could almost picture was long gone now, replaced by more utilitarian carpeting that had since faded so badly I could no longer guess at its original color. And it was worn through in places, permanently stained by spills of unknown origin in far more.

The original hand-turned wood of the banisters was still there, though. If dinged and scarred now, the last coat of polish long since worn away leaving a sticky residue from the passage of countless human hands and the accumulation of decades-worth of dust.

But enough details remained to paint me a picture of Gilded Age luxury. I almost wanted to set my box down, dig out my sketchbook, and make that mental picture a physical one. Alas, now wasn't the time.

We reached the third and final floor, then followed Jesús and Tlalli to the left, to the very end of the corridor and the last door, again on the left. Tlalli unlocked the door and then held it for all of us with boxes to precede her inside.

Cozy was definitely the first word that came to mind as we crowded into the apartment. And I'm not being sarcastic, either. Yes, it was a very small space. But Tlalli had truly gone all out with furnishing it. It was, in all honestly, a cozy little nest for two.

The window that dominated the far wall of the room framed a glorious view of the autumn trees atop the ridge to the west. The couch that sat below the window was covered in a throw blanket in stripes of scarlet, gold, amber and topaz that subtly echoed that view. Weird how that made the space almost feel bigger? Like the outside world was part of it?

The kitchen was tiny, but exceedingly efficiently organized, the shelves over the sink already filled with enough cups and dishes for not just Kara and Thorge alone, but for guests as well.

And the coffeemaker was already brewing a pot of fresh coffee, filling the air with the welcome aroma of lightly roasted beans.

There was no dining area or even a kitchen table, so meals would have to be eaten from the couch or from the two straight-backed wooden chairs that flanked it. But the coffee table all of those seats were gathered around was large and sturdy, a perfect square of solid wood that had recently been polished to a gorgeous shine.

As I set my box down against the wall, I could just catch a glimpse of the bedroom on the north end of the room. It was a tight space, barely large enough to contain the double bed that was meant to go there. But it had windows to the west and north, and like the window in the main room, they were of very generous size and offered incredible views.

Since moving to the North Shore more than a year before, I was now the owner of not one but two entire homes, one in the heart of Villmark and the other a cabin in a clearing completely surrounded by woods. And yet I couldn't help feeling a little pang for another, older dream I had had, of one day having my own place in the city.

Granted, this was back when I was still going to school, and the city I had imagined living in had been St. Paul. Or if I was really dreaming big, Chicago. But still.

"This is really nice," I said, finishing my thought out loud.

"It is," Kara agreed. "Thank you so much for all you've done, Tlalli."

"Don't mention it," Tlalli said with a flush to her cheeks. "But we're not quite done yet. Jesús and I were just trying to work out how that bed frame goes together. We got it secondhand, so there aren't any instructions."

"We thought it would be obvious," Jesús said. "Alas."

"We shall work something out," Thorbjorn said, with the same grim determination he brought to patrolling the borders of Villmark and keeping all his people safe from threats like trolls and giants.

Thorge just nodded, then followed his brother into the bedroom to examine the various pieces of bed frame that Tlalli and Jesús had left strewn across the floor.

"There's a mattress?" I asked, not seeing one.

"It's in the closet," Jesús said. "It's the one thing we got brand new. Well, that and the pillows. But it comes vacuum-sealed inside a plastic bag. Once we open that up, it's going to make doing anything in that room very difficult."

"Once the frame is assembled, we can open it up," Tlalli said. "But it has to expand for something like 24 hours before you sleep on it, so we also scrounged up some air mattresses and sleeping bags for tonight."

She looked extremely anxious as she gave us that news, but before I could even summon a response, Kara—who seemed to recognize the source of Tlalli's worry at once—said, "After months sleeping in the back of a wagon, anything indoors is a luxury for me still."

"I've heard of air mattresses," Thorge said from the bedroom, mere feet away. "I've always wanted to try one."

"Prepare to be underwhelmed," Jesús said. Then he stepped into the bedroom to explain everything he and Tlalli had already tried in regard to that bed frame.

"That coffee smells so good," Kara bemoaned as she sat down on what was now her couch. She settled back into the cushions and gave an approving nod, then shifted to look out the window behind her.

"I made some decaf for you already," Tlalli said, producing a metal thermos from amongst a tidy gathering of canisters and pouring out a steaming cup for Kara. "Cream or sugar?"

"We have those things already?" Kara asked.

"I stocked your fridge with the basics, but you'll want to do your own shopping soon enough, I'm sure," Tlalli said. "Don't worry, I have tomorrow off too. I'll walk you around the neighborhood and show you the closest grocery store as well as the clinic you'll be going to for your appointments, although I fully intend to go to all of those with you too. But I want you to feel comfortable on your own if you have to."

"You've really thought of everything," I said, giving Tlalli another quick hug. "The guys are busy, so I'm going to run back down to the car and fetch those last two bags."

"I can help you," Kara and Tlalli both said at once, then laughed.

"I'm fine," I assured them both, motioning for Kara not to get up from the couch. "It's just two bags. I'll be back in a jiffy."

"Wait," Tlalli said before I had quite reached for the door back out into the corridor. She dug into her pocket and then produced a pair of keys on a single ring. "I made an extra set of keys for you, just in case. The one with the red dot on it opens the lobby door, and the one with the silver dot is for the apartment door. The red one also opens the door to the alley, and the silver one works on the laundry room door down in the basement, but I can go into all that later."

"Got it," I said, stuffing the keys into the front pocket of my jeans. Then I went out the door, back towards the stairwell.

I could just hear Kara saying, "Laundry room?" as the door clicked shut behind me.

I was so grateful that Tlalli was going to be there. I hadn't thought of even half of the things that were going to strike Kara and Thorge as strange and new.

But it was okay. They were going to be okay.

I jogged down the steps to fetch those last two bags.

CHAPTER THREE

I WENT OUT through the lobby, but as I walked back to where I had parked the car, I realized that it would've been quicker to go out the back way. There was an alley behind the apartment building, but a large one. No lakes of ooze gathering under the single dumpster back there. No shadowy corners for malcontents to lurk. Perfectly safe.

I opened the hatch of my Volkswagen and reached for the bags, but the minute I grasped their handles I realized they were far heavier than I had anticipated. Heavy and awkward both, each of them catching on a dozen unseen protrusions in the back of my car, fighting my efforts to wrestle them out. I finally got one out and slung it by its handles over my shoulder so I could use both hands to grasp the other.

This didn't exactly work out. They were gym bags, but the long, adjustable straps I might have used to sling them across my body weren't attached. There were only the shorter hand-carry straps, which I could just squeeze my shoulder through if I wasn't super concerned about blood flow down to my hand.

The straps bit painfully into my shoulder, but still always seemed precariously close to slipping back off again. I shifted my body 45 degrees to my right to keep the bag I had on my left shoulder secure, and that worked just long enough for me to get the other bag out. I set it at my feet and slammed the hatch closed again, but I didn't see a way to get that bag up onto my right shoulder. Every time I tried it, the left started slipping down again, and I had to set the right bag back down and adjust.

I know what you're thinking. Take two trips, right?

Yeah, I'm stubborn. I didn't want to go through all this a second time. I didn't even want to start fishing my keys back out to open the hatch again. That all seemed like too much of a bother.

Instead, I grasped the second bag by its straps and left it in my hand. I could get most of the way upright now, one bag on my left shoulder and the other dangling from my hand almost down to the rough, undoubtedly sticky surface of the road. Like that, I still couldn't stand fully upright, but I could just manage a 30-degree tilt, like the bag in my right hand was a sort of counterbalance to the one on my left shoulder.

I looked both ways, then when I saw it was clear, I started shuffling across the road. Technically jaywalking, but my only path now was the most direct one I could take. I crossed the road at a bit of a diagonal, then continued along the same line, straight into that alley.

As much as I had already noticed the lack of a lake of dumpster juice or signs of drunks peeing in the corners of the space, I was still surprised at the smell as I carried on putting one foot in front of the other. It took me a moment to place the smell, which was so very out of place.

It was gingerbread, I was sure of it. But there wasn't a bakery anywhere near where I was standing. I risked a glance up at the windows of the buildings to either side of me, but none were open. And anyway, why would anyone be baking gingerbread two days before Halloween?

Although a gingerbread haunted house did sound like a pretty cool idea. My mind was already working out how to fabricate sufficiently scary trees out of black licorice. And candy-coated chocolate in purples and browns would make a suitable front walk...

My train of thought completely derailed as the bag on my shoulder started slipping again. I caught it in time, but when I tried to hike it back up again, it was catching on the sleeve of my shirt, bunching it up in a way that really wasn't helping my blood flow problem.

"Do you need some help, dear?" someone asked me. I didn't quite jump, but I had been pretty certain I was alone in that alley. My situational awareness—combined as it was of both my physical senses as well as my magical ones—was usually too thorough for anyone to sneak up on me, even the Valkissons, who could stalk deer in their soft-soled hunting boots.

And yet, even as I struggled with the two heavy bags, a woman had appeared right at my elbow, clucking worriedly at me. She was very old, and very tiny, but she didn't look frail. Her back was straight, and the hands that fussed over me were steady and strong. She was a little overdressed for the weather in what looked to be a man's wool coat, the kind that would get super heavy if you tried wearing it in the rain. The sleeves were threatening to swallow up her hands, and the hem showed stains of all the things it had been dragged through as it brushed the ground around her feet.

It took a certain amount of strength to just carry all that wool around, plus whatever was bulging out the line of her pockets.

Still, I wasn't about to hand her either of the bags. I was fairly certain that either one of them outweighed her by quite a bit.

"I'm okay," I said, although the work it took to get those words out undercut my message more than a little. "I don't have much further to go. Just to that door there."

With both of my hands occupied, I resorted to pointing with my chin.

The woman followed the direction of my point and said, "Ah," in a way that sounded like she had never seen that door before in her life. Like it was a surprising new feature. "I would offer to get the door for you, but I'm quite certain that it would be locked."

"Don't you live here?" I asked her. Because I was pretty sure the windows I could see on the second story of the building next door to the apartment building all opened out from office space above the retail stores on the street level. And I couldn't see a single other reason for this woman to be in the alley that ran between the two buildings.

"Nearby," she said vaguely. "Are you moving into this building, dear?"

She spoke that question with an intent look in her eyes, like she was deeply concerned what my answer might be. Did she think I was breaking in or something? I mean, who breaks into a building already loaded down with heavy bags? If I looted anything, how would I possibly carry it back out?

"No, my friends are," I said. "But I have a key."

"That's not what I mean," she said. Then she took a step closer to me. The top of her head barely came to my shoulder, but she grasped my arm for balance as she whispered up as close to my ear as she could reach, "That place is haunted. You should tell your friends."

I almost told her I didn't sense anything, but that would steer the conversation into territory I really didn't want to try navigating with a stranger.

Plus, I was distracted by something else. The gingerbread smell that permeated the alley? It seemed to be coming from her.

"Ghosts?" I said, mostly playing for time.

"Of course, ghosts," she said as she stepped back to her original position. Which was still awfully close to me given that we were strangers to each other and both clearly descendants of Scandinavians, a people not known for being close talkers. "What else haunts a place?"

"Oh," I said. But that was a whole other can of conversational worms I wasn't looking to open.

But then, to my surprise, the woman literally threw her head back and laughed. At first, it sounded self-deprecatory, but then it edged into a cackle that was on the verge of spinning out of control before she stopped as suddenly as she started and beamed a smile up at me.

"I was only fooling with you," she said with a mischievous gleam in her eye.

One that suddenly had me missing my friend Loke all over again.

"I won't go inside that building since I don't live there, but if you give me your key, I'll help you get inside. Those bags look very heavy."

"They are," I admitted, and gratefully set one down so I could dig the ring of keys Tlalli had given me out of my pocket. They tangled with my car keys momentarily, but then came free. "It's the one with the red dot," I told her as I flexed my hand a few times before picking up that bag again.

It hadn't gotten any lighter.

"So it is," the woman said, and carefully took hold of just that key, keeping the others tucked in her palm as she advanced on the heavy steel door. It was a fire exit, the kind that automatically shut tight when not held open.

Whoever this woman was, I was glad she was there to help me out. I would've had quite an ordeal, getting two bags through a door that wanted to shut itself as badly as this one wanted to. The woman had to brace her whole back against it, hands on her knees to keep herself steady as she held the door.

I slipped the left-side bag off my shoulder to hold the straps in my hand where I had better control. The last thing I wanted to do was barrel her over by mistake.

I set them both down inside the corridor on the other side of the door. I could see lights spaced adequately along its length, but they were so dim compared to the bright autumn day even in the alley behind me that the narrow space felt dark and spooky.

But not haunted. Not to my senses, anyway.

"You're stronger than you look," I said to the woman as I put a hand on the door to hold it open so she could step away from it.

"Always have been," she said proudly. Then she handed me back my keys. "I do hope your friends stay safe in there. I don't like to speak ill of the dead, but I have never liked that place."

"The ghosts are bad ghosts?" I asked.

The woman said nothing in return, not for a long time. But I could tell that she was chewing on the inside of her cheek, like she was debating what to say.

And I could see something I was sure was fear in the wideness of her blue eyes.

But then she just gave herself a little shake and a smaller laugh than before. "I'm being silly. Never mind me. I know Halloween is mostly a commercial thing these days, a fun day for the kiddies. But when I was young, it was something very different. Something much darker."

"Some of us still keep to the old ways," I said before I could quite pull it back. Halloween wasn't a thing in Villmark at all. We did have a variety of harvest festivals, because who didn't love to gather to share a bounty with a huge feast? And we had a lot of ways of dealing with the dwindling of sunlight leading up to Jule, when finally the nights started getting shorter again and we came back into the light of spring.

But the only thing I had seen that had made me truly afraid was the Wild Hunt. And it was still weeks away from the time when those fell riders roamed the world at large.

Whatever the woman thought of my words, she didn't say. She just grunted an acknowledgement upon hearing them, then turned and walked away.

The scent of gingerbread lingered behind her. And yet she carried nothing on her, no basket possibly filled with baked goods, nothing. Unless the pockets of her wool coat were filled with cookies, I couldn't explain the smell of her at all. I mean, I know people make perfumes now in scents like gingerbread, but they always still have a chemical tang that gives away their artificiality.

The woman's scent had none of that. She smelled for all the world as if she had just spent the last eight hours baking pan after pan of gingerbread.

I stuffed the keys back in my pocket, then took up the bags again with a sigh. I didn't have the strength left to try to get either one of them up onto my shoulder a second time, but I didn't have much further to go, really.

Sadly, the only way to get them up the stairs at all was to lift them a little higher, so they didn't bump every step on the way up. I was really getting a workout in today for sure.

Only three more flights of stairs to go. Just one step at a time.

CHAPTER FOUR

I MADE it up a single flight of stairs before I had to set the bags down again and take a break. I wasn't even on the second floor yet, since the back and forth on the back stairs was tighter and had landings between the floors.

I wiped the sweat from my brow and was just bending to grasp the straps again when a voice in the murky dimness above me said, "You met Gladys."

I knew it was only murky dimness because my eyes still hadn't adjusted after coming inside, and no one was lurking there in the dark trying to freak me out on purpose.

But for just half a second, I thought I was being addressed by one of the old woman's ghosts.

Then I blinked, and a shape emerged. A teenage girl was sitting on the top step, tucked almost under the banister as if she didn't want to be in the way of anyone using the steps. Although from the layers of dust on the concrete around me, I would say this staircase didn't see much use.

She was definitely real and not a ghost. She had a tablet computer perched on her knees with a stylus currently twirling through her fingers, and I didn't think there were many ghosts around who could drag modern technology into the afterlife with them. Plus, the T-shirt she was wearing featured character art from an animated movie that was currently taking the world by storm, so if she was a ghost, she was very recently dead indeed.

Which was a morbid thought. So I just said, "Gladys?"

"The old woman who helped you in the door," the girl said. Then she turned her attention back to the tablet, ceasing the twirling of her stylus to make an adjustment to something I couldn't see on her screen.

"She seemed harmless," I said.

"Oh, she is," the girl assured me. "She scares some of the little kids in the building, but not on purpose. She just doesn't have a good sense of boundaries, I think."

I could see where that would be true. But the girl's attentions were now firmly fixed on her tablet. She was rotating and zooming in and out with her left hand while she made strokes with the stylus in her right hand. It was a workflow I was very familiar with, although it had been more than a year since I had done any digital work.

But now I had two reasons to pause again where the stairs met the second-floor corridor. I set the bags down and then sneaked a glance at the image on the tablet over the girl's shoulder.

She was sketching herself, to judge from the long waves of auburn hair the figure on the screen sported. But this version of her was wearing a tall hat over that hair, as well as a knee-length dress with a full skirt over tights and boots.

The cut of the dress wasn't necessarily witchy, but the stripes on the black and white tights and the laces on the pointy-toed black ankle boots totally were. And yet the colors of the dress—red with large white dots—as well as the mushroom shape of the hat, which was also red with white dots, evoked a more fungal image.

"Character design?" I asked. Her style was very clearly drawn from anime and manga, but there was a flair to it that was all her own. Which I was kind of envious of. I was a lot older before I even started to look like my work was my own and not just copies of someone else's.

"No," she said with a nervous giggle. "This is going to be my Halloween costume. I'm going to a party."

"And you can make that in two days?" I asked.

"I think so," she said, the fingers on her left hand nervously zooming the image in and out. Then she rotated it a bit and added another dot to the skirt. "I have a red dress that's pretty close to this. I can sew on some white dots, I'm sure. And the tights and the boots my friend Lina is going to lend me, since she doesn't want to be a witch this year. The only problem is the hat. But I have to have one to make the dress make sense."

I squatted down beside her to examine her drawing more closely. "Do you only need it to hold together for one night?" I asked.

"Yeah," she said, but warily. Like she'd just realized she was chatting with a stranger who might not have benign intentions.

"Make a frame out of cardboard strips," I said, then gestured for her to hand me the tablet. She thought about it for half a second, then passed it over to me. I sat down on the lumpy surface of one of the bags and opened a new layer on her digital painting program, quickly turning off all the others she had been drawing on so that I had a blank page on the screen to work with. "One strip goes around your forehead, like a band. Then make a cross across the top of your head to hold it on, right?"

"Okay," she said, still skeptical.

"Then add a ring like a flat doughnut. That's the brim," I said, sketching it in. "It looks like a gardening hat now, right? But all you need is some cream-colored cloth, like even cheesecloth, to glue to the bottom of the ring. Do you have a hot glue gun?"

"My mom does," she said, brightening now. "I think I see what you're doing."

"Right," I said, even as I continued sketching out the way the mate-rial would bunch into folds, like the gills of a mushroom. "Then you cover the top side with red fabric or felt, whatever. If you stuff the inside, it will look fuller."

"I can do that," she said. "Then white felt for the spots. That's what I was going to use for the dress. I already have it."

"One more hint," I said, finishing up my construction drawing for the mushroom hat with a few more flourishes with the stylus. "Use just a little bit of stuffing under the white spots. Not too much or the hot glue won't hold, but just enough to make them bump out a little. It's the little touches that really sell the whole look."

"And on the dress too," she said, suddenly breathless with excitement. "I can do this. Thanks!" She took her tablet back and got up, but stopped herself before she'd quite started scampering down the corridor. She thrust a hand out at me and said, "I'm Hailey, by the way. I heard you tell Gladys it was your friends moving in, but I hope I see you around again."

"I'm planning to visit a lot, so I'm sure we'll meet up again," I said, shaking her hand. "I'm Ingrid."

"It was good to meet you, Ingrid," Hailey said. Her words were almost stilted in their formality, a girl remembering her manners. But the grin that went with them was entirely genuine.

Then she was gone, her sneakered feet pounding down the carpeted hallway. I was pleased to find I could see all the way to the far end now, so my eyes were done adjusting.

I hefted the bags up once more and carried on to the next flight of steps. I wanted to power through to the very top, but once I reached the landing between the levels, I knew that wasn't happening.

I set the bags down again and wiped my brow. I hoped that, in addition to the coffee, Tlalli had stocked the fridge with something cool and refreshing. Although at the moment I would be grateful for nothing more than lukewarm tap water.

I was just about to pick the bags up again when something made the hair on the back of my neck stand on end. I felt a cool draft wash over me, but as much as my brain wanted to put those events in the usual order, I couldn't lie to myself. I had felt goosebumps first, then the draft. Not the other way around.

I turned to look back down the stairs. There was no central well here, just a wall that divided the stairs up to the third floor from the stairs back down to the second floor. It was completely impossible for me to look all the way down to the first floor.

And yet, I had the strong sensation that someone was down there, looking up at me.

Someone, or something.

The feeling left as quickly as it had come, and my mind wanted to dismiss it entirely, but again I didn't allow my brain to lie to me. I knew what I had felt.

Well, I didn't know what it *was*, but I knew something had happened.

I toyed with the idea of going back down to check, but dismissed it. The feeling was gone, so whatever caused it was likely gone as well. And I didn't want to leave the bags unattended, even in this space that showed clear signs of never being used by living humans.

And I definitely didn't want to bring them with me.

Still, I had more than a few questions for Tlalli spinning around in my mind when I finally reached the apartment door. I was over-joyed to find it standing ajar, but it hadn't been left that way just for me.

There was a visitor in the apartment, a middle-aged woman with dark blonde hair in a shoulder-length cut so severe I suspected she trimmed it herself. She was wearing a hand-knit sweater vest covered in a leaf motif, a complicated pattern created by a very competent knitter.

The woman turned as I nudged the door wider open with one foot and smiled at me. "Here she is," she announced to the others.

"Yes, here I am," I said, stumbling into the room and then setting the bags one by one in the most out of the way spot I could find. Which wasn't too terribly out of the way at all. Anyone trying to get back out of the apartment was going to have to climb over them. Oh well.

"Ingrid, this is Karen, my new next-door neighbor," Kara said almost proudly. "She brought us a plate of brownies and some very lovely homemade lemonade."

"I always buy more lemons than I know what to do with," Karen said with a dismissive wave at the compliment. "I just love the smell and the color, don't you? It's like holding sunshine in your hand."

"Indeed," I said. Tlalli put a chilled glass of lemonade into my hands, and I downed it in an embarrassingly short amount of time. But it was just what I had been longing for: something cool and tart and not too sweet. "That just might be the best glass of lemonade I've ever had," I said.

"Pish posh," Karen said with another little wave. "You just carried those two bags up all those stairs. That works up a thirst."

"You're not wrong," I conceded, but handed my glass back to Tlalli so she could fill it again from the nearly empty pitcher. She poured the last few drops into the glass in front of Kara, then took the pitcher to the sink to rinse it clean.

"I'll just take that and then get out of your hair," Karen said. "But feel free to stop by anytime you need anything at all. I'm always home now that I've retired, and I promise you it's not any trouble. I love having something useful to do."

"Thank you so much," Kara said.

Karen just gave little waves to each of us and then headed back out into the corridor, letting the door click shut behind her.

"You're beet red," Tlalli said to me. "You should've taken two trips."

"I had a little help," I said. "There was an old woman in the alley who helped me get in through the fire door."

"The alley?" Kara repeated, aghast for no reason I could see.

"Yeah, why?" I asked.

Tlalli shrugged, but there was something ever so slightly performative about her unconcern. "Before Karen came over, we were chatting with a little boy who lives on the first floor. It seems he came up here on his own just to warn us about the back door."

"What about the back door?" I asked. "I mean, it was very heavy and awkward to get the bags through, but—"

"He said the corridor down there is haunted," Kara said. "And maybe the alley too? It wasn't entirely clear."

"He left in a hurry when Karen approached with the lemonade and brownies. Didn't even stay for a brownie. So maybe he was just telling stories," Tlalli said. But then Kara turned away to set a plate in her sink and Tlalli shot me a significant look. She didn't think the boy was lying, that was clear. But she clearly didn't want to alarm Kara by saying so.

It was always possible the boy was speaking from the heart, telling the truth, and was just wrong about what was happening. But before I could try for more silent communication with Tlalli, Kara turned back around, drying her hands on a dish towel.

"Haunted by what?" I asked instead.

As much as when I had said something similar to Gladys, the only answer had been obviously ghosts, that wasn't the case with my friends. We had seen all sorts of things.

"I would say nothing," Tlalli said at last. "I've been down there myself, bringing things out to the dumpster. I have never sensed anything. I think it's all just a story."

"We mentioned it to Kara, and she says all the kids insist the alley and the downstairs corridor are haunted," Kara said. "They wind each other up, she said. The weird thing was, she kind of admitted none of the adults go through there either. Everyone uses the front door, even if it means more walking. And she kind of dodged our questions when we pressed. So we stopped pressing."

"The hallway is dark, especially after coming in from outside. And the building is old," I said, nodding. "Still, I wouldn't think ghosts would be here."

"So far north?" Tlalli asked teasingly.

"Well, all things considered, this town isn't terribly old," I said.

"Does it have to be, to have ghosts?" Kara asked, completely seriously. "All you need for a ghost is a restless spirit, right?"

Tlalli scrunched up her face and made something like an "eh?" sound.

"I don't have any experience with ghosts myself," I said. "Or, at least, not the kind that appear in ghost stories. Not 'traditional' ghosts," I added, making the air quotes.

"Nor do I," Tlalli agreed. "And I've been on a few of the haunted tours around town since I moved here. I've been to the Glensheen

Mansion with some school friends, and Jesús and I have both checked out the Duluth Depot and the Duluth Public Library. Actually, he's been to the library a bunch of times. It's a cool building." She shrugged.

"Those are all haunted?" I said. "I mean, I heard about the murders that took place at the mansion, obviously. But murders don't necessarily mean ghosts. If they did, the world would be overrun. Sadly."

"Well, it's a tourism draw," Tlalli said. "On a smaller scale than, say, all of New Orleans. But still."

"This place was a hotel once, right?" Kara said. "Were there any murders here?"

"I haven't done any research like that," Tlalli said. "But I've been up and down both staircases more than once. I haven't been up and down the first and second floor corridors, but I've been up and down the third floor, and all over the main lobby and the laundry room. I never sensed anything."

Kara thought this over, then nodded. She knew Tlalli's skills as well as I did. She was satisfied with this answer. She leaned forward to pick up her glass of lemonade and drain the last of its contents.

But I was still a smidge curious. I looked over at Tlalli, who was gathering empty glasses, the remains of some break the bed-making trio had taken while I was still making my way to the car and back, I assumed.

"Have you ever seen a ghost?" I asked. "Or anything like it?"

Tlalli straightened with two glasses clutched in each of her hands and cast her eyes up and to the right as if scanning her memory.

"Not as such," she said slowly, each word distinct.

"Not, as Ingrid said, 'traditional' ghosts?" Kara asked, mimicking my air quotes.

"No," she said. "I've felt things, though. In places that were supposedly haunted. Not here, in Duluth. But in St. Paul in a few places, and more so in my home in Mexico City. Not distinct entities, so maybe I wouldn't even call them ghosts?" She shrugged before heading to the kitchen sink to wash the glasses.

I followed her, pulling the kitchen towel from where it was looped through a cabinet drawer pull, preparing to dry what she washed so we could keep Kara's kitchen as tidy as she'd found it.

"What *was* it like?" I asked.

She didn't seem to hear me at first, like she was engrossed with the motions of washing four glasses in the sink and rinsing them clean before handing them to me, one by one. I wiped them dry and then lined them back up in their places in the cupboard over the stove. Then I handed the towel to Tlalli so she could dry her own hands.

She made a thorough job of it. Then she shook out the towel before threading it back through the drawer pull. Only then did she cross her arms and look at me.

"It's not like a person, so I wouldn't call it a ghost," she said. "What I've felt in these places, it was more like the memory of the place. Like strong emotions from humans long gone left an imprint. But it's like a strong smell left behind after something rotten has been removed. Unpleasant, but not actively harmful."

"But you didn't sense that here?" I pressed.

"Did you?" she countered.

I remembered that feeling on the stairs. But that hadn't felt like the memory of strong emotions or anything like that. It had just been an out-of-sequence experience, like time had run backward for a split second.

Was there a word for that? Something like déjà vu?

"No," I said at last. "I think this building is just like any other. A bunch of bricks and stone, with some modern amenities running through it. Nothing more."

"If you both say it's fine, then I'm sure it is," Kara said, then stretched back on the couch like she desperately wanted a nap.

She probably desperately needed one. This day was a lot for her, I knew.

But as much as I still had a niggling worry about what I'd sort of sensed before, it was easy to set it aside. Because if there was one thing I knew was true, it was that Kara was far more sensitive than I was. And she hadn't felt anything at all.

As long as that remained true, I wasn't going to feed any worry monsters in my mind.

Especially not two days before Halloween. Unlike the Villmarkers, I had grown up with a spooky season. And I might not be a kid anymore, but I still was more prone to jump-scares this time of year.

I joined Kara on the couch, and the two of us shared a doze in the warmth of the afternoon sun streaming in through her glittering window.

CHAPTER FIVE

EVENTUALLY, the bed frame was assembled, and the mattress was released from its vacuum-packed confines. Tlalli and Jesús had evening shifts to get to, and I'm sure Tlalli had schoolwork on top of it that she wasn't admitting to. After they left, the four of us had a quick meal of canned soup and grilled cheese sandwiches before Thorbjorn and I finally had to say our farewells to head back to Villmark.

"Text me if anything unusual happens," I told Kara. "Anything at all."

"I will, I promise," Kara said, giving me one last goodbye hug.

And yet still I lingered there, unwilling to leave despite the lateness of the hour. I wanted to stay. But it wasn't physically possible. Until the mattress had enough time to puff up to its full dimensions, Kara and Thorge would be sleeping on the living room floor. And there was barely room for two to do that. Four would be entirely out of the question.

"Right," Thorbjorn said, as if sensing my trouble. He slipped an arm around me and gently pulled me out of the cozy apartment. "We'll be getting out of your love nest now."

Thorge chuckled as he closed the door behind us. Then Thorbjorn and I were alone together in the murky light of the hallway, and he dropped his carefree facade at once to look at me gravely.

"*Do* you sense something? Something we should be guarding against?" he asked.

"No," I said. But I couldn't be less than fully honest with him. "There was something, maybe, at the bottom of the back stairs. But the woman I met in the alley was going on about ghosts, so I think she just gave me the creepy-crawlies."

Thorbjorn mulled this over. Then he took my hand, guiding me not back to the front lobby but to the very end of the hall, where the stairs to the back door were.

After reaching the bottom of the stairs, I still saw nothing. Nothing more than our two new sets of footprints were marring the single set I had made in the previously untouched dust. The only thing I was sensing was the buzzing of the fluorescent lights and the urge to sneeze from the dust we were kicking up. Nothing else. No half-seen things lurking in the shadows, no whispery sounds of lurking things moving about surreptitiously. Nothing.

"Did you want to draw this place?" Thorbjorn asked after we had lingered a long, silent minute at the bottom of the stairs.

"This entirely unexceptional staircase?" I asked in what I hoped sounded joking.

"You know what I mean," Thorbjorn said.

"No," I sighed. "I already reached out with all of my magical senses several times. There's nothing here. And besides, it's late. You have patrol in the morning."

"Something I've done with little sleep on many previous occasions," he pointed out.

"Fine, but you're not doing it this time. Not on account of my jumpy nerves," I said. Then, I laid a hand on his arm. "Come on. We'll go out the very spooky back way. And once that ends up being entirely uneventful, we can make the equally uneventful long drive home."

Thorbjorn nodded and then led the way to the back door. It took a bit of effort to swing it open. Besides being generally heavy, I suspected the hinges were rusty as well. Not surprising in view of how seldom used this back way apparently was, but certainly not ideal in a fire door. People would need to get out this way in a hurry, potentially.

I made a mental note to text Jesús about getting after that bit of maintenance. Then Thorbjorn and I got into my Volkswagen and headed north.

It was fully dark long before we got home. I parked my car in its new spot in the driveway of my grandmother's recently rebuilt cabin, but all the lights inside were dark, so I knew she wasn't home. Which made sense; at this hour she would be in her mead hall.

But I opted not to stop in. By now, Kara would've texted her, as well as her own mother and her sister Nilda and probably Loke's little sister Esja as well. No one was waiting for an update from me.

So Thorbjorn and I walked past the quiet front of the building that appeared to be any small town's municipal center, little more elaborate than your average pole barn, really. Then we continued on past the slightly less quiet back of the building, which at this time of day looked like a proper Viking long house with heavy timbers and a thatched roof, all of it giving off a subtle golden glow.

What was the building really? Well, it was both at once. It looked different from different angles, and through different people's eyes. But my grandmother stood with one foot firmly planted in the lost Viking village of Villmark and another foot equally firmly planted in Runde, Minnesota. It only made sense that the business that was the entire focus of her life would reflect the same characteristics. Not of contradictions, but of an unexpected and yet thoroughly logical unity of her two worlds.

We could hear voices raised in laughter and in song, and the beat of a modern dance track thumping repetitively followed us long after the rest was drowned out by the babbling of the river beside us, just out of sight through the tall grasses.

Then the babbling became a roar as the path we were following reached the bottom of a waterfall. Our route briefly became more of a climb than a walk as the trail through the boulders beside the waterfall went nearly vertical before leveling out again in a narrow track that disappeared behind that cold curtain of water.

The cavern directly behind it was always a magical place, dark and sandy, but with the silvery light from the rising moon broken by the water into a thousand dancing motes. Like from a disco ball, as if the light itself were dancing to the beat that we could no longer hear.

The deepest point of this cavern was a narrow cave, a massive stone always standing ready to be rolled in front of that cave in defense, a measure that was almost never necessary to keep Villmark safe. And past that stone was the cavern where we kept the ancestral fire, a fire that had been burning since the founding of this village so many centuries before by the witch Torfa.

Thorbjorn's father, Valki, was on duty tending to the fire, but he only briefly greeted the two of us before waving for us to continue on our way.

I guessed I looked as worn out by the day as I felt. And it wasn't just lugging the boxes and bags up the stairs. No, when you get out of the habit of driving a car every day, you forget how much work it is, always being aware of your surroundings and being prepared to react defensively if need be. To suddenly go from months of no driving to spending more than five hours in one day behind the wheel was exhausting.

Luckily, it was a short walk from where the cave opened up again in the midst of the meadow at the top of the waterfall, through a stand of birch trees whose branches were largely bare now but whose fallen leaves made the walk both an auditory and olfactory delight, to the first cobblestoned road of Villmark proper.

My townhouse was just south of the main square which was the village commons. But we didn't have to walk that far before my six-toed black cat Mjolner joined us. He gave me a slightly chiding meow, as if pointing out the lateness of the hour, then fell into step beside us for the rest of the walk home.

It was well past ten by this point, and on a weeknight, although that didn't matter much to most of the people of Villmark. Even so, I could see the lights were still on inside my house, and when Thorbjorn opened the door, it was to find both of my housemates, Roarr and Esja, waiting for our arrival.

Esja was Loke's little sister, although the family resemblance between the two of them was something maybe only an artist's eyes could see. It was in the line of their cheekbones, the slight pointiness to their chins, the shape of their ears. It absolutely wasn't in their coloring. Loke was all dark hair and chocolate brown eyes, standing out starkly against his paler than pale skin. But Esja's long hair was white-blonde, her eyes a cornflower shade of blue. It was true, once she had been as pale as her brother, back when she had been sickly and housebound for most of her days. But now that she was healthier, she was outdoors so much of the time that even now, at the end of October, her skin still glowed a sun-kissed shade of bronze.

Esja was living with me while her brother was away up north. At first this had been necessary because, basically, her body kept getting hijacked by some mysterious power that manifested like the three Norns of mythology. Which had been scary for all of us. But even now that it was all past, she stayed as my guest.

She didn't want to go back to her family's farm in the hills south of Villmark. Not without her brother. And I couldn't blame her. Besides, as a fellow artist, I found she was the best kind of company.

Roarr, who had appointed himself my assistant of sorts and then Esja's guardian of sorts, was technically only a half-time roommate. He had moved in when Esja was having the hardest time, because he could sense better than I could when whatever that thing had been was working through Esja. Now that the thing was gone for good, neither Esja nor I really needed him around. And he knew that, and so he split his time between the spare room in my house and his room in his parents' house.

And honestly, I had come to rely on him more than I would've ever imagined I could. He had been so helpful, particularly through the long, lonely months when both Thorbjorn and Loke had been up in the north. Now that Thorbjorn was back, though, I still liked having Roarr around.

At the very least, he did a better job than either Esja or me of remembering to do the shopping. And, having once been engaged to a girl from Runde, he understood the greater world better than anyone save perhaps Loke. He even looked like any guy from Runde, wearing faded Levis and a heavy flannel shirt over a navy blue waffle-weave thermal undershirt. The slip-on leather shoes he wore indoors were thoroughly Villmarker, almost like moccasins without the beadwork, but the socks were the traditional Midwestern warm outdoorsy kind, thick gray with red toes and heels.

My roommates. The two of them didn't even pretend to be subtle about the fact that they had been waiting for me to get home. My front door had an entryway with a bench to sit on when getting out of shoes, and hooks for outerwear from light jackets to heavy parkas. But past that was just a corridor. It was a good ten feet to get to the kitchen door, and further than that to get to the living room. But there the two of them were, leaning against the wall at the top of the three steps up from the entryway itself.

"Kara texted us when you left her place," Esja said.

"And I told her this was the earliest we could expect you back," Roarr added. "I showed her the map on her phone that calculated the driving time, and that was assuming you didn't make any stops on the way."

"We didn't make any stops," Thorbjorn said.

"Are you hungry?" Esja rushed to ask. "Roarr and I had potato soup for dinner, and there was plenty left over. I can heat some up for you?"

"We ate before we left," I said.

"But thank you," Thorbjorn said. Then he yawned hugely. "Sorry. Clearly, all I need is a warm bed and a few uninterrupted hours in it."

"Of course," Esja said. "I wished I could've gone with you."

"I, too, would like to see Duluth again," Roarr said.

Because he had been there with me once before, when the trail of investigating the murder of a Villmarker woman had led us so far afield.

But I had a hunch what he had really wished was to see Tlalli again. He had danced with her at Kara's wedding, months before. And

I was sure I had seen sparks between them. Although whether they had kept in touch with each other afterward, I honestly didn't know.

But it was far too late at night to start that kind of prying.

"There was only room for four in the car, sadly," I said. "And I already promised Nilda and their mother that they would be on the next trip down."

"Maybe some other time, then," Roarr said. If he was disappointed at all, he hid it well. But then, his emotional state was often a mystery to me.

"Absolutely," was all I said.

Roarr stepped back to make room for Thorbjorn, who was making a beeline for the bathroom upstairs to start getting ready for bed. Roarr lingered uncertainly for half a moment, then he too headed up the stairs.

"I know I've only been gone for a matter of hours, but how are you doing?" I asked Esja.

"I'm all right," she said, too cheerily. I gave her a stern look, and her cheeks flushed. "I'm not lying. I really am fine. At least in the ways where you all have to keep an eye on me. Roarr was here all day, after all."

"And in the ways we don't have to keep an eye on?" I pressed.

Esja bit her lip briefly then sighed. "I don't know. I guess maybe I thought, Kara and Thorge leaving and you and Thorbjorn just being away for the day, that was a pretty big event."

"You thought it would bring your brother home?" I asked.

She scowled, but in a way that told me that, as much as she hated to admit it, I had hit the mark exactly.

"He'll be home," I assured her.

"You don't know that for sure," she said.

"Esja," I said softly. "You and I both know that if anything truly awful happened to your brother, we would both sense it. We *know* that, don't we?"

She bit her lip again, but just nodded in reply.

"As long as nothing truly awful has happened to him, I think we know he's not here because he isn't finished with what he went into the north to do. And until he's finished with that, we just have to be patient."

She nodded again, but a little less sorrowfully than before.

"And being patient definitely sucks as an activity," I said. She rewarded my attempt at a joke with the smallest of chuckles.

"That's true," she said. "It really does."

"So tomorrow, find something else to do with your time," I told her. "Me? I think I'll start with sleeping in a bit. And then enjoying not being in a car."

I gave her shoulder an affectionate rub, then headed up the stairs, Mjolner trotting just at my heels. Once I was out of earshot of Esja, though, I looked down at my cat.

My cat, who had appeared by magic into my life just as I was about to leave St. Paul, although I hadn't known it yet. My guardian angel through so many adventures. He could walk through walls, he could augment my magic or disrupt the magic of others if needed to protect me.

He could also, I was quite sure, speak. But so far it was only Loke who could hear him, although Roarr understood him better than me in some strange way.

Mjolner's green eyes looked back up at me as I regarded him.

"You'd tell me, right? If Loke was in trouble? You'd lead me to him so I could help him. Right?"

Mjolner, of course, said nothing. But he blinked those lantern-bright eyes in one long, slow blink.

Which I knew meant yes. If Loke were in danger, I would know.

But whatever was keeping him away from us for so long? That, I couldn't know. And, like being patient, accepting not knowing was hard.

And yet, what else could I do?

CHAPTER SIX

I woke up the next morning feeling all out of sorts.

I had succeeded in my goal of sleeping in. From the angle of the sunlight filling my room, I guessed it was mid-morning already.

But that meant Thorbjorn had slipped out without waking me. And while Mjolner was still there, curled up on my pillow with his spine pressed to the back of my neck, his vigorous sleep-purrs vibrating my entire skull... Well, it really wasn't the same.

Yet that wasn't what was wrong. That was, in fact, an all too common occurrence in my life. I loved Thorbjorn with all my heart, but his calling as protector of our village was just as strong as mine to be the volva of our people. And protecting the village meant long hours—days at a time, really—away from me. That was just part of the package in building a life with him. I always felt a little pang when I woke to find him gone, but it was a pang I was used to.

No, something else was bothering me, if only subconsciously. I threw an arm over my eyes to shut out the golden light and let my brain settle back into a liminal state.

And almost instantly got my answer. I had woken from a dream, a disturbing one to judge from the images that were washing back over me now.

A dream about that alley, behind Kara and Thorge's apartment building.

I was still trying to make the images coalesce into anything beyond eerie vibes when the sound of my cellphone vibrating on my bedside table disrupted the process. Ignoring Mjolner's meow of protest, I sat up and grabbed my phone. Tlalli's name was on the screen, and I answered the call just before it would've shunted to voicemail.

"Tlalli?" I said. "Is everything okay?"

She didn't answer right away, which was probably answer enough. But then she did speak, if hesitantly. "I honestly don't know." Then she seemed to realize how that sounded and rushed to say, "Kara and Thorge are both fine. I've already spoken to Kara. No worries there."

"But?" I prompted, rubbing tiredly at the back of my neck.

"Maybe it's nothing," she said.

"No, you called me for a reason," I said.

"Yeah," she said. "Look, I don't know about you, but I don't really have prophetic dreams."

"Like telling the future? Me neither," I said.

But I suddenly really wished I had remembered more of whatever I had been dreaming about just minutes before. There had been a feeling, an unsettling feeling. But I couldn't remember why. I had been in the alley, I knew that. But what had I dreamed I had seen?

"But you sometimes get magical information in your dreams, don't you?" Tlalli asked.

"When I'm trying to bond with a rune and it's not working out, sometimes sleeping on it helps. And I get dreams with a lot of symbolic stuff going on. But I don't think that's really *prophetic*," I said.

And tried not to feel guilty about putting off working on my latest rune until after I had gotten Kara and Thorge settled. I was going to have to get on that now.

Of course, the rune I was working on now was Jera, which represented the end of a year. Don't think I wasn't tempted to use that as an excuse to push it back until December. Only I still had so far to go to master all the runes, which I had to do before I could properly call myself a volva. I couldn't exactly afford to take it more slowly. My grandmother was doing better now than she had been a year ago when I had just arrived, but she was still getting older. I had to be ready to step up when she couldn't carry on anymore.

But I pushed all those thoughts aside to focus on pulling more words out of Tlalli. "You had a dream, I take it?"

"Nothing symbolic, like what you're describing," she said. Then she blew out a sigh. "I'm being silly. I'm sure it was nothing."

"Nothing, like a 'standing in the alley behind the apartment building feeling deeply uneasy but not knowing why' kind of nothing?" I asked. "Like you don't see anything that should make you feel so in peril, and yet you do?"

I listened to Tlalli breathe for a moment. Then she said, "You dreamed it too."

"I don't remember much, but that's the gist of it," I said.

"Does *that* mean anything? The fact that we both dreamed it?" she asked.

"I honestly don't know," I said. "Did you even go down to the alley?"

"Not yesterday, but I've been back there before," she said. "I've been in some creepy alleys in my day. That one was definitely not on my list of creepy alleys."

"No, me neither," I said.

"Maybe it's nothing, then," she said.

"Yeah, but neither of us believes that, do we?" I said drily.

"So, what do we do?" she asked.

Now it was my turn to heave a mighty sigh. Because I knew I was about to spend another long day in the car.

"I'll drive down," I said. "But I don't see getting there any sooner than two."

"I have classes today that I absolutely can't miss," she said. "But if you start drawing when you get here, by the time I join you maybe we'll have something to work with."

"What kind of work are you thinking of?" I asked.

Not that I ever didn't come prepared. I always had my art bag with me. And my bronze wand always lurked there, at the bottom of that art bag.

"I'm texting with my mentor Saoirse Duncan now," Tlalli said. "She's from a Celtic tradition, if you remember. The thinning of the veil at this time of the year is very much her kind of thing. Maybe what we're sensing is just related to that. I mean, if the building really is haunted, even just by memories, they're probably stronger now than usual. Stronger memories, but that doesn't necessarily mean dangerous."

"No, I'm not sure I was dreaming of danger," I said, half-closing my eyes in another futile attempt to dredge up a memory. But the dream had faded already. "Unease, yes. Eerie vibes. But I don't think danger."

"Yeah, but we want to be sure, right?" Tlalli said. "Look, I have to get to class now, but I'll see you this afternoon, okay?"

"Absolutely," I said.

I washed up, dressed, and shoved some food in my mouth. Then I headed out the door, art bag over my shoulder.

I was halfway out of Villmark before I realized that Mjolner was there with me, trotting along at my heels.

"You're coming too?" I asked.

He just meowed as if annoyed I was even asking. When we reached my car, he jumped inside, turning around three times before curling up to sleep on the passenger seat. He didn't so much as stir during the entire ride to Duluth. But once I had parked on the steep road south of the building, almost the exact spot where I had parked the day before, he stood up, stretched in that contemplative way that cats do, then joined me in crossing the street to reach the alley itself.

The first thing I noticed was a distinct lack of eerie vibes. It was just an alley, paved ground between two not even terribly tall buildings. The sky was intensely blue and almost cloud-free, although it was late enough in the year for the position of the sun even this early in the afternoon to be decidedly southerly.

The second thing I noticed was a lack of gingerbread smell. So, had it all been coming from Gladys the entire time? I supposed that was a possibility. But the smell had been so intense, like it was coming from an entire gingerbread factory. And, as I had noted before, she hadn't been carrying anything that might've been hiding even a much more modest amount of gingerbread.

But the lack of a cheery aroma hardly made a sun-filled alley eerie.

"What do you think?" I asked Mjolner.

He looked around intently, sniffed one corner of the dumpster, and crept along one of the brick walls as if on the hunt. But it appeared to be a fruitless hunt. After watching him explore for a few minutes, I settled down on the concrete stoop of the apartment building's back door and took out my sketchbook.

The last page with drawing on it had been from after I had talked to Haraldr, my mentor in learning the runes. It was filled with the off-center pair of pointed brackets that represented Jera, the rune representing the end of a cycle of time. The end of one cycle, the beginning of the next. Basically, time itself. It came after the three runes that were associated with the three Norns, who were the past, the present and the future.

In one way, it really did fit the end of the calendar year, when everything in the modern world sort of resets. But it also fit this time of year, because one of the things it represented was the reward for hard work. Namely, the harvest after a good year. The end of October was really the end of the cycle of harvests that started months before, when the first fruits ripened on the trees.

I retraced one of the Jera runes I had drawn before, the brackets that flowed one into another. It was a rune that couldn't be reversed, because reversed it looked just the same. Summer flows into winter, then back into summer again. Nature takes its time, but eventually everything else emerges from that flow. The opposites of fire and ice that, at least in Norse thought, existed before all other things still managing to work together in the creation of all those other things.

It was the very farthest thing from a bad omen, is what I'm saying.

So I turned the page, put Jera out of my mind, and started drawing the alley around me.

By the time Tlalli joined me, I had a dozen sketches of the alley. I had drawn it from both ends, as well as from various points in the middle. I had even taken a blanket from my car and spread it on the paved ground so I could lie down and draw it from that angle.

Mjolner, I swear, chuckled cattily at that. But I had done it all the same.

But examining the sketches afterward, all I saw were the mundane features of a perfectly normal alley running between two perfectly normal buildings.

"Maybe we should try drawing in that hallway," Tlalli suggested after she, too, had examined all my drawings for possible clues and come up empty.

"Did you dream of the hallway?" I asked.

"No, but that's where I get the strongest sense of memory ghosts," she said.

I shrugged. "It couldn't hurt. I've been at this for an hour, and I really don't think I've missed anything."

Mjolner meowed his agreement. Well, he had been hunting the entire time I was drawing. Although whether he was hoping for a sign of a ghost or was merely looking for a nice city rodent to play with, I wasn't entirely sure.

I sat on the bottom of the dusty staircase, from where I could see the full length of the hall ending in that fire door. Mjolner sat beside me, fussily bathing himself although the most dirt he had been exposed to so far was the dust on the step where he was sitting now, so that was a pointless exercise.

Tlalli was doing something with her wand, something that struck me as maybe an attempt to peer through that veil between the world of the living and the world of the dead. But none of her words meant anything to me, and I didn't want to interrupt her to ask. So, I just focused on moving my charcoal pencil over the open pages of my sketchbook.

When I came out of my fugue state later, it was to find Tlalli no longer doing anything other than watching me sketch. I looked up at her, but she shook her head. She had found nothing.

I looked back over my drawings. I had leaned in heavy on the shadows, but there was no denying this was a very dark space. There were lights spaced evenly along the length of the hallway, but they could definitely use a brighter wattage of bulb.

I traced my already blackened fingertip over the textures in those shadows, but there was nothing hiding there. Not in my sketch, and not in the hall. Not that I could perceive, anyway.

"I'm sorry I made you come all the way down here because I had a feeling," Tlalli said, rolling her eyes at her own expense.

"No, I had the same feeling," I said as I packed my art things back into my bag. "I'm glad I came. I suppose you have work again tonight?"

"You know it," Tlalli said, then glanced at the time on her phone. "And I'm late. Terrific."

"I'm heading upstairs to see Kara and Thorge before I head back home," I said, taking two steps up the staircase to do just that. But then I turned back to catch Tlalli before she'd quite gotten back out through the heavy door. "If you have another dream or anything at all, please call me. Don't second-guess yourself. There's something here we don't understand. I don't think it's *dangerous*, but I don't like not understanding things. Okay?"

"Absolutely," Tlalli said. "But that goes both ways."

"You only beat me at calling because you woke up sooner," I promised her.

Then we exchanged waves, and I headed up the stairs to the third floor, Mjolner at my side.

But I kept mulling over that last thought. Because I had been entirely honest on both counts.

I *didn't* think it was dangerous, whatever we were feeling in our dreams.

But I really didn't like that I didn't understand what it was.

One way or another, I would rectify that.

CHAPTER SEVEN

AFTER A QUICK DINNER with Kara and Thorge, where Kara caught me up on how her first appointment with the OB/GYN had gone, Mjolner and I headed back up to Runde.

I told myself that everything appeared fine. The apartment building hadn't shown any signs of being a danger to anyone, and neither had the alley. Kara had already gotten over any of her worries about living in the city, and had genuinely bonded with the woman who was going to be her doctor throughout her pregnancy and delivery. If Kara ended up needing specialists, this woman was still going to be with her all the way. That was an important relationship, and I was very relieved it was starting out on a good footing already.

Still, as I fussed about getting ready for bed that night, I knew I was nervous. The dream I had been having the night before had been the furthest thing from a nightmare, though. So why was I so on edge about what that night would bring?

Mjolner was with me, for one. Having been caught in actual magical nightmares I had needed his aid to escape from, that was reassuring to know. He didn't seem on alert in any way. He was just a kitty planning on stretching out on my pillow all night long. As much as he adored Thorbjorn, he had been letting me know in various cat ways that sharing bed space with anyone besides me was absolutely not his favorite. But he was going along, out of deference to me.

So, I thought my cat's presence that night was more about the two of us being alone than any worry about me getting trapped in my own dreamscape. But all the same, I made an extra effort to work at sketching the Jera rune over and over before finally turning in.

I told myself I was just trying to be efficient, focusing on making a connection with that rune. But the fact that it was a rune with no reversible, dark side was definitely a factor.

I slept late again, but this time dreamlessly. I awoke to find the sun halfway up the sky, but with no memory of anything that I might have been dreaming just moments before.

I got dressed, then headed down to the kitchen to make coffee and toast. Mjolner padded alongside me down the stairs, but no one else appeared to be home. That wasn't unusual, either. Roarr had been with his parents the night before, and Esja often spent her days out and about Villmark rather than stuck at home.

She had had decades of being trapped in a house by her ill health. I didn't begrudge her any opportunity to get out when she could. Especially with the weather holding out so fine, warm and sunny.

I found coffee waiting for me in the carafe, just enough for one cup, which was all I usually wanted. I put some bread in the toaster, then turned my attention to my phone.

And saw several texts from Kara. I gave them a quick glance, but before even processing any of them, I switched over to the phone and called her directly.

"Ingrid," Kara said breathlessly, answering with such speed on the first ring that I was sure she had been clutching her phone in her hands, waiting to hear from me.

"I just woke up," I told her. "What's going on? You said you and Thorge are fine, but something has you upset."

"It's Karen. Do you remember Karen?" she asked.

"Your next-door neighbor," I said. "The one with the brownies and lemonade."

"Right."

But when she didn't go on, I had to press. "Has something happened to her?"

"I don't know," Kara said. "You were here yesterday for a reason, right? I mean, you were hedging when I asked, but you and Tlalli were both here, down in the alley and in the back stairwell. Hailey saw you."

"Yes, but I wasn't trying to be secretive," I said. "We just wanted to double-check some things. But there was nothing there to worry about. That's the only reason I didn't bring it up. It was, well, sort of a false alarm. If you can say that about something that wasn't even alarming in the first place."

"You said we were safe here," Kara said, but not in an accusatory sort of way. No, it sounded more like her personal mantra, like an affirmation she had been repeating a lot.

"What happened to Karen?" I asked again.

Kara sucked in a breath, but pressed on. "She seems to have gone missing. She went out last night to pick up a few groceries before dinner, but she never came back. Her husband, Michael, has been beside himself, checking with the police and calling all the local hospitals. But so far, there's been no sign of her. The clerk at the grocery store didn't remember seeing her, so she maybe never even made it that far. She certainly never made it back home again."

"I'll be back down," I said at once.

"Tlalli has classes and work all day today, so I didn't want to bother her," Kara said. "It's such a long drive for you, though. And alone, right? Thorbjorn is still out on patrol."

"He is," I agreed. And, looking around, I realized I had lost my cat as well. "I'll be down as quickly as I can. But I'll go grab Roarr for company on the road if it makes you feel better about the driving."

"I know you're perfectly safe—" Kara started to say.

"Doesn't mean that traveling with company isn't still a good idea," I interrupted. "I'm going to pack up and head out now. But text me if you hear anything about Karen in the meantime, all right?"

"I will," Kara said.

I double-checked my supplies in my art bag, decided to grab a second empty journal because the one I had been using was down to a handful of blank pages, then called one last time for Mjolner. But when he didn't appear, I headed out on my own, walking at a speed that was almost a jog to the west end of town where Roarr and his parents lived.

His mother, Ragna, didn't seem surprised to see me. She just gave me a tight hug, inquired after my grandmother's health, and then sent me on back to the kitchen.

Where Roarr was just finishing up the last crumbs of a cinnamon roll in the company of Esja.

"Oh, you're both here," I said, a little taken aback. I mean, I had come down to my own kitchen to see the two of them gathered together there dozens of times. I'm not sure why in this house the entire scene felt more intimate. Like I was intruding.

But Esja just produced another cinnamon roll from a covered basket at the end of the table and put it on a plate before handing it to me.

"Sorry, I was up with the sun again this morning," she said as she gestured for me to join them at the table. "I went to sit with Nilda by the bonfire for a while, but then I just had this niggling feeling like I was meant to be somewhere else. But that was a maddeningly vague feeling to try to act on. After wandering the streets aimlessly for a while, I decided to just get a little brunch since I'd skipped breakfast. And having brunch meant finding my brunch buddy. And so here I am."

"If you needed us, volva, I think we know Esja followed her feelings correctly. She was meant to be here when you arrived," Roarr said.

Which, I supposed, was entirely possible. Esja still had something of magic in her, although it wasn't a variety I or my grandmother understood very well.

But it might just come in handy.

"I was actually only looking for Roarr," I admitted before biting into my cinnamon roll. So much better than the dry toast I had forgotten upon seeing Kara's messages. "I need to go back to Duluth today, and I was hoping you'd come with me."

"Of course," he said.

"But not me?" Esja asked.

"Well," I said, "that's up to you. I'm planning to be back before nightfall, but I know how you feel about watching out for your brother's return. If being in Duluth is too far away for you, I'd understand. But, everything else being equal, I would like to have you with me. Just in case you see or sense anything I don't."

Esja folded her arms and dipped her head down as she mulled it over. I watched her worry her lip between her teeth as I finished off the last of the cinnamon roll, then waved off Roarr's offer of more coffee.

Finally, Esja looked up at me, her blue eyes grave and intense. "I wasn't joking, you know. I really felt this morning like I needed to be somewhere. And I really think that somewhere is with you. I would like to go. Even though Duluth is, as you say, very far away."

"I'm ready to go when you are," Roarr said. "I would like very much to see where Kara and Thorge are living."

"Then let's head out," I said.

Although I was going to have to stop for gas first, having just made it home the night before on what was left in the tank.

And I was all too aware of how short my funds of modern-world money were growing. I had gotten through art school without taking out loans, through a combination of scholarships and grants as well as working full time while taking classes, so it could be worse, I knew. But I had been forced to sell my childhood home in St. Paul to pay my mother's final medical bills and funeral expenses. I had moved north with almost nothing to my name, and that situation hadn't exactly improved when I had started living and working entirely in Villmark.

I was going to have to redouble my efforts to submit illustrations to book publishers for sure. And in the meantime, I should whip up more pen and ink drawings for my friend Jessica to sell in her café beside the highway. That would at least keep me in gas money for a while longer.

I just hoped that whatever was going on in Duluth, it would stop needing my daily attention soon.

Although with a woman mysteriously missing now, I was definitely doubting that was going to happen.

CHAPTER EIGHT

IT WASN'T EXACTLY SURPRISING, the fact that Roarr and Esja both dropped whatever they had planned for the day to join me on a trip to Duluth and back without even knowing why I was going there. Although, given the sorts of things I usually asked them to assist me with, they were probably expecting we were going to see a dead body.

So on the walk down to where my car was parked in Runde, I explained who Karen was and why Kara was worried about her.

But I didn't say anything to Roarr or Esja about the alley or the back hallway of the apartment building. I wanted them to pass through both areas completely cold. I needed to know what struck them without any idea that I was looking for them to sense anything at all.

I honestly expected the two of them, or at least Roarr, to have a lot more questions for me. But I had forgotten to take into account that this was the first time Esja had been further out of Villmark than my grandmother's mead hall. The sight of the homes of the fishing families of Runde tucked under the tall pines along the rocky shore of the lake was enough to quietly wow her.

Then I pulled out onto the highway, and I knew for a fact she had never traveled anywhere as fast as my Volkswagen was going. And its old engine was straining to keep up with the speed limit. Cars and trucks were constantly blowing past us.

Roarr spent most of the trip twisted half around in the front passenger seat, drawing Esja's attention to various things along the way. It's a scenic drive with plenty for anyone to see, especially at that time of year. He also pointed out places like the Split Rock Lighthouse, Palisade Head and Gooseberry Falls as we passed them. Not that we could see much of those from the highway without stopping.

Which reminded me just how little I knew of Roarr. He had been engaged to a young woman from Runde named Lisa, but she had died the very day I had come to live with my grandmother, so I had never met her. Still, he had been intending to leave Villmark to live with her. And she had been going to school in Duluth at the time. I knew he had been there before he had gone with me, but I had no idea his travels up and down the North Shore had been so extensive.

But mostly what he was pointing out to Esja were very mundane things, like business logos and billboards and the bumper stickers on other cars. He got a nervous giggle out of her a few times, and I realized that he had sensed something that I had not.

Esja was terrified. She was holding it together, but she was extremely nervous about this trip.

I wanted to tell her it would get easier, but if she hadn't let me see that she was even nervous, it was probably better to make her think she was hiding it better than she was. It was enough that Roarr was comforting her anyway.

And it effectively created the situation I wanted. When I finally parked my car in what was fast becoming my usual spot, neither of them was the least bit suspicious when I led them across the steep road and into the alley behind the apartment building.

Well, neither of them had enough experience with apartment buildings to know that it was more usual to use the front lobby. And I had the key to the back door. So why would they be suspicious?

But after passing through the sunlit alley to the back door then down the shadowy hall to the staircase that was starting to lose its coating of dust with the constant passage of my feet, and still neither of them had said anything, I couldn't take it anymore. I felt compelled to prompt them.

"Anything weird about this place?" I asked as casually as I could as we made our way up to the third floor. "Do you sense anything off? Anything at all?"

"You think something we could sense is what took this Karen woman?" Esja asked, suddenly looking around more intently than before.

"I noticed nothing," Roarr said with a tone that swore he had been paying attention.

"Tlalli and I made a thorough search for anything out of the ordinary just yesterday, so I guess that's not surprising," I said. But I was still disappointed.

But then Roarr said, "Esja?"

And I looked over at Esja, who had a ponderous look on her face.

"Did you sense something?" I asked, drawing us all to a halt at the top of the stairs.

"Nothing magical," she said. "But you said anything weird at all, right?"

"Right," I agreed. Although frankly, given this was her first time in the city, wasn't everything a little weird to Esja?

Still, Roarr pressed. "What did you sense?"

"There was a smell, in that back alley," she said. "Like gingerbread. Is that normal?"

"Not for this time of year," Roarr said confidently. But then he shot a look at me. "Right?"

"It's a little out of season," I said. "I didn't smell it today, but I did two days ago. I think maybe there's a bakery near here. Or someone in one of the apartments is getting an early start on their Christmas baking. I don't know."

"That's all I sensed," Esja said with a shrug. "Do you want me to go back down and try harder?"

"No, let's go see Kara first," I said.

Kara answered my knock at their door at once, as if she had been standing there waiting for me. She was momentarily surprised to see

Esja as well as Roarr with me, but couldn't ask any pointed questions about it, as there was a stranger on the couch behind her.

The man was late middle-aged with neatly trimmed, if thinning, gray hair. He was dressed like a college professor down to the shapeless sweater with elbow patches, but not even the voluminous folds of that faded sweater could cover up the fact that he was in very good shape for his age. I suspected he ran marathons, or at least trained to run them. He was that kind of lean.

Not that I was about to inquire into his workout regime now. I could see from the redness of his eyes that he had gotten no sleep since the day before and was fighting back tears even as he rose to shake my hand in hello.

"You must be Michael," I said as I settled into one of the straight-backed chairs. "I met Karen the day before yesterday, but only briefly. I know she's been very kind to Kara and Thorge. I'm sorry for what's happened."

"Whatever *has* happened," he said with keen frustration.

"Ingrid is going to figure out what happened and where Karen is," Kara said with absolute conviction.

Which only made me clear my throat nervously to say, "Well, I'm certainly going to try."

"I'm not sure what you can do," he said.

"Why don't we start with what you know, and I'll see where I can go from there," I said, taking a sketchbook out of my bag as well as a graphite pencil. I usually worked in charcoal, especially on these exploratory sorts of sketches, but I didn't want to explain my process in that moment, so I stuck with what would be more familiar to him. I wanted it to look like I was just taking notes. Even so, I kept the book perched on my drawn-up knees, the page out of his sight.

Not that I needed to be so guarded. He sat back on the couch, his hands to his face in what I took at first to be a moment of restrained emotional response, but which turned out to be his method of refining his recall.

At last he slid his hands down enough so that I could see his eyes, but his gaze was fixed on a random point on the table in front of him. Like all he was truly seeing was the past.

"She had made a lasagna for dinner," he said. "This was about five or so. She had just put it into the oven. But it was a new recipe, and she was worried about how it would turn out. Not that she'd ever served anything that was less than fabulous. But she worried like that. So she decided to go down to the bakery on the corner, to get some of their rosemary and olive oil bread. In case the lasagna was a disaster, you see. We could have the bread with the leftover cheese and tomato sauce from the lasagna."

"So you last saw her at five last night?" I asked, even as my hand kept itself busy, sketching Karen from memory. I couldn't recall her face very well, though, and the sketch was mainly focused on a jug of lemonade with condensation coating the glass in a way that was making me thirst for that cool, sweet beverage all over again.

"Yes," he said, dropping his hands from his face to press the fingertips together, like a lecturer about to make a point. "But someone else saw her after that for sure. Hailey Tvedt saw her as she was heading out to the store."

"Hailey lives on the second floor, right?" I said as I turned a page and started a fresh sketch of Hailey.

"Yes, but she often babysits for a few of the families in the building, so it's possible to run into her almost anywhere," Michael said. "But this time she was on the first floor when she saw Karen."

"In the lobby?" I asked.

"No," Michael said. "No, that's what's odd. She didn't go out through the lobby. For whatever reason, she went out the back way. But Karen *never* goes out the back door."

"But Hailey saw her there?" I asked.

"Yes. They exchanged brief hellos, then Karen went out the door into the alley. And *that* was the last time anyone saw her," he said.

"She never made it to the bakery?" I asked.

"None of the clerks remembers seeing her. And there's nothing on their security cameras," Michael said. "She just went out the back door into the alley and… disappeared."

"Right," I said, closing my sketchbook. Nothing I had just drawn was giving me the sense that it contained any hidden clues, so there was no reason to linger on the images now. "I'll start at the back door, then."

Michael nodded, then fell into a sort of reverie. Roarr nudged Thorge and whispered something in his ear, and Thorge suddenly came to life. "Michael, why don't I walk you back to your apartment? You should try to get some rest."

"Yes, we'll come at once if we learn anything at all," Kara assured him as she, too, got to her feet. She and Thorge helped Michael out of their tiny apartment, leaving the door open as they went out into the hall.

But they were far enough out of earshot for Roarr to whisper to me, "You already knew it was the door or the alley, didn't you? That's why you asked those questions before."

"I suspected," I said. "Tlalli and I both dreamed about the hallway and the alley the night before last. Nothing about disappearing people or anything sinister at all, though. And when we came back to look more closely, we found nothing at all."

"I'm so sorry," Kara said as she rejoined us, closing the apartment door behind her. Thorge was still with Michael, apparently.

"Sorry for what?" I asked, genuinely confused.

"It's my fault Karen is gone," she said. "Like Michael said, she never went out that back door. No one in the building does, although aside from the kids telling stories of ghosts, I don't think any of them could explain to you why. But after you and Tlalli left yesterday, I was chatting with Karen in the hall, and I told her you both said that area was perfectly safe. I was just trying to put her mind at ease. I didn't think… well, I didn't think any of this would happen."

"That's a good argument for it being my fault, not yours," I said. "But we don't know what happened yet. I'm going to go out and draw the alley again, and maybe check out that bakery too."

"You think the clerks at the bakery are lying about not seeing her?" Kara asked with a frown.

"No, I doubt that," I said. "But if I retrace her steps, or at least the steps she had intended to take, maybe I'll find something."

"We'll go with you," Roarr said, and Esja nodded.

"Me too," Kara said, but I was already shaking my head at her.

"No, I have a different job for you," I said. "I need you to find Hailey. I met her briefly on the day we moved you in, and she struck me as a very observant girl. I'd love to talk to her myself about what she saw before Karen disappeared."

"Of course," Kara said.

"We won't be gone long," I said, then led Roarr and Esja back out the door.

"You didn't tell her why you really want to go to the bakery," Esja said the minute the door had clicked shut behind us.

"What do you mean?" Roarr asked, confused.

But I knew what she meant. "Well, I can at least see if they sell gingerbread," I said. "Not that I think it's any kind of clue to Karen's disappearance. But I'm curious why I keep smelling it in the air."

Then we jogged back down three flights of steps to the alley door.

CHAPTER NINE

I DREW the back hallway again. And the doorway itself. And the alley beyond. I drew them from every possible angle, poring over each sketch when it was done in a vain search for clues.

But all the time I was furiously getting the charcoal lines down on the page, with Roarr hovering around like a bodyguard on high alert, Esja was sitting shoulder to shoulder with me. She had brought a sketchbook of her own, although she was working with colored pencils. Which made sense. She generally preferred to work in watercolors, but our constantly shifting positions and the pace of the work would've made that difficult and potentially messy.

Well, the charcoal all over my hands and right forearm wasn't exactly *neat*. But paint and water would've been a lot to tote around. Although I'd seen some little travel-ready watercolor kits with water pens, and I would have to pick one up at some point to see how Esja liked working with it.

In the meantime, she was turning out some lovely work with the colored pencils. Alas, her drawings were as free of clues as my own.

I had to catch someone passing on the street to figure out which way to walk to find the bakery. But I knew as soon as they pointed the way that it wasn't going to be the solution to my gingerbread question. The bakery was downwind of the alley. It couldn't be the source of the smell.

And after Esja and I had spent a quarter of an hour drawing there, I didn't think it was relevant in the search for Karen either. So we were back to square one.

At least, when we got back to Kara and Thorge's apartment, Hailey was there waiting for us.

And she was wearing her mushroom dress, complete with mushroom hat. It was only then that I realized that today was Halloween. With all the driving back and forth, I'd completely lost track.

"That came out lovely, didn't it?" I said, admiring the hat and the dress both.

"Yes, thanks for the advice on the hat," Hailey said, ducking her head just a little in a shy, nervous gesture.

"You are going trick or treating?" Roarr said, enunciating the words a little too distinctly, which only made his usually all but invisible Villmarker accent stand out starkly.

But Hailey didn't seem bothered by it. "Actually, I'm going to a party. All the kids I babysit are going out with their parents this year, so I'm not needed for that."

"I won't keep you," I promised. "I just wanted to ask about when you saw Karen yesterday."

"I already told Michael all about it," Hailey said, but not in a way that was dodging my question. It was more like this was the first piece of information she was offering me. "I was babysitting on the first floor at the time. The Olsons. They're pretty young, three and five now, so I was letting them play with their cars in the hallway. Chasing the cars around burns off a lot of steam, you know?"

I had never worked a babysitting job a day in my life, and was an only child on top of that. But I had a certain amount of experience with kids that age from serving tables at the diner since I was in high school, so I just said, "I know."

"Right," Hailey said. "We weren't in the stairwell or anything, but I was standing right by it in case I needed to keep a stray car from careening down that way. You know, away from the corridor that leads past all the apartment doors and into that back hallway that none of us ever use. The kids are a bit scared of it. That's why I was there when Karen came down."

I nodded, encouraging her to continue even as I pulled out my sketchbook again. She looked at it with keen interest, and I remembered she was something of an artist herself. But she didn't ask me about it. She just carried on with her story.

"At first, when I heard someone coming down the stairs, I thought it must be you. Because you and your friend are the only ones I've seen use it at all. But it was Karen. I could tell she was in a hurry, so I didn't say more than a hello to her. She said the same to me, and I saw her digging in her pocket as if she were double-checking she had her keys. Then she went out the door."

"And you didn't see what happened after that," I said. Flatly, because it was more a prompt than a question.

"No, it was very sunny outside, and very dark inside, so when she opened the door it was like I was blinded until it shut again," Hailey said. "But I really don't know why she went that way. No one ever does."

"Why not?" I asked, as casually as I could.

"We just don't," Hailey said. But, as if she didn't need prompting from me to recognize that wasn't a helpful answer, she frowned in thought. "Look, the kids say it's haunted, but that's obviously nonsense, right?"

I said nothing.

So she took a breath and then went on. "I can't speak for anybody else, but the place just gives me the creeps. I don't know why. As far as alleys go, it's clean and really kind of nice? And with all the pavement away from the streets, it would be a great place to bring the kids to play. It's a couple of blocks to the nearest park, and with the traffic on the roads around here, I don't like to be the one walking any of the kids there."

"But you've never played in the alley?" I asked.

"Not even once," Hailey said. "I've been living here since I was a baby. But not even once did I play in that alley."

"And when you say it gives you the creeps, can you elaborate on that?" I asked. "Do you feel like you're in danger, or like someone is watching you, or just like someone is hanging out back there?"

"No, none of those things," Hailey said. "It's just... creepy. Like something isn't quite right. It doesn't feel dangerous exactly. Just, not right." She ended with a shrug, clearly giving up on trying to dredge up more from her own impressions.

"I know what you mean," I told her. "I've felt the same way since I saw it. But no matter how I've analyzed my own feelings, I don't know why it's creepy."

"It just is," she agreed. But then she glanced at the time on her phone and gasped in alarm. "I'm going to be late to my party."

"Do you want us to walk you?" I offered.

"No, thanks," she said even as she adjusted the hat on her head and started for the door. "That *would* be weird, showing up at a party with a trio of strange grownups." She chuckled, then seemed embarrassed by her own reaction. "No, I'll be okay. I'm going out through the lobby, and it's broad daylight out there, anyway."

"Okay, then. Have fun!" I said.

I hoped I didn't sound as worried as I felt. Because I knew whatever teenaged party she was heading to, it would surely be dark before it ended and she started walking back home.

But also, I couldn't help remembering that Karen had disappeared in broad daylight.

"Now what?" Roarr asked after Hailey had left.

I could feel Kara's eyes on me as she anxiously awaited my answer.

"I don't know," I admitted. "I had quite forgotten that today was Halloween."

"Does that matter?" Esja asked.

"I know it's not really a thing in Villmark, but it's a magically important time of year. In many traditions, this night is when the veil between the world of the living and the world of the dead is thinnest. Given that the only real reason anyone has ever given me for avoiding the back hallway is that it might be haunted, this day may be significant to what's going on here."

"Ghosts kidnapped Karen?" Kara asked with a frown.

"I don't know," I said again. "I just want to hang around and keep an eye on things, at least for tonight. Do you mind?"

"Having company? I'd love it," Kara said at once. "We have enough bedding for the three of you to camp out in here, although the couch is going to be a tight squeeze even for Esja. And you and Roarr would have to share the floor. But we still have the air mattresses."

"Not a problem," Roarr said without hesitation. "Let's keep a vigil for any ghosts, then drive home in the morning."

"I'm in," was all Esja said.

"It's not much of a plan," I admitted, even as I pulled out my phone to text my grandmother.

Thorbjorn's schedule for when he returned from patrols was always up in the air. It varied depending on whether he had found anything that needed more attention or not. But it was just possible he might come home to find me missing. And while I was sure Mjolner could find a way to convey where I was to him, it would be far easier if I just asked my grandmother to pass a message along.

Kara forced the three of us to sit down and eat a plate of sandwiches before she'd let us head back down to the alley. And I was grateful for that later, when I realized that the vigil I had only partly planned out was truly going to have to be all night long if it was to be at all meaningful.

Esja marveled at the costumes on first the children and then the adults heading for parties or clubs who passed on the sidewalks at either end of the alley. Roarr just sat with his back against the door, holding it open so that I could see both locations from my position on the stoop.

Then even the adults had all wandered back home to bed, and only the three of us remained. I sketched a little, but I wasn't sensing a thing. And even Esja wasn't smelling gingerbread anymore. Roarr let himself doze off, uncomfortable as his position as a doorstop must have been.

I closed my eyes, not to sleep but to cast out my magical awareness. But I felt nothing. Maybe because there was nothing to feel, or maybe because, as a volva, this wasn't the right time of year for feeling the thinning of the veil. In the Norse traditions, that happened at Jule, when the night was longest and the day was shortest.

On that night, the dead really did walk. Or rather, they rode with the Wild Hunt. I had been out in the open when they had passed by, and I had very narrowly avoided being taken with them, never to return.

But nothing like that happened in that alley on Halloween night. The stars spun overhead, and the moon trudged from one end of the sky to the other.

And then the sun started to rise, although I couldn't see it from the alley itself. But when the sky overhead started to turn pink, I accepted that nothing supernatural was going to happen that night.

I nudged Roarr awake, then touched Esja's shoulder. She had been standing all night long, looking towards one end of the alley or the other tirelessly. She didn't jump at my touch, but it still felt like I was summoning her back from some other place deep within her own mind.

I just gestured towards the third floor of the apartment building, and she nodded. Roarr stumbled to his feet, not quite losing his hold on the door. Then the three of us trudged upstairs, slipping into the apartment as quietly as we could.

Kara had left the mattresses and sleeping bags out for us, and Roarr and I each silently took one as Esja settled on the made-up couch. I slipped out of my shoes and crawled into the bag, punching at the pillow until it formed a more comfortable configuration.

Then my eyes slid shut, and I hoped, I desperately hoped, that all that awaited me was dreamless sleep.

I got my wish in the sense that I didn't have a single memorable dream that night.

But, alas, that wasn't all that awaited me. Not by a long shot.

CHAPTER TEN

I'M sure most of the reason I didn't remember anything I might have dreamed was that it felt like I had only just closed my eyes when I was opening them again.

But some time must have passed, because what woke me was the sound of Kara and Esja coming in the apartment door. And when I had shut my eyes, they had both been tucked away in their respective beds. Or rather, one in a bed and one on a couch. But either way, my eyes must have been shut for more than the few seconds it felt like.

Although not nearly long enough to call what I had been doing "sleep." I sat up, shoving tangles of hair out of my face. The inevitable result of sleeping tucked so deeply down inside a sleeping bag. The only thing fiercer than those tangles was the static electricity making every loose end float.

I was momentarily distracted from the aches of sleeping on a now half-deflated air mattress and the general exhaustion of everything by the smell of freshly baked croissants. When was the last time I had had a croissant? Flaky and buttery and warm. And I was sure I was detecting the aromatic undertones of chocolate in there as well. I was going to kiss Kara and Esja for their breakfast-procuring skills.

But then I saw their faces. And the offhand way that Kara dumped the bag from the bakery on her counter, turning her back on it without even opening it up.

"What happened?" I asked. I had already gleaned they'd been to the bakery. And I could tell from the logo on the bag, it was the one in the neighborhood where Karen had gone. Which made their solemn expressions all the more concerning.

"There's been another disappearance," Kara said.

Roarr beside me sat up at once, running his hands through his thick dark blond hair. On one pass he had his just below the ears waves neatly arranged, and his face and eyes were alert, like he had already had his morning's coffee.

I was pretty sure my face was puffy and my eyes red-tinged from lack of sleep. Not to even mention the snarls of my hair.

But I pushed those worries aside. "Who?" I asked.

"Hailey," Esja said, and my heart clenched in my chest.

"What do we know?" I asked, even as I fought my way out of the sleeping bag and reached for my shoes. "She went to that party last night."

"She was going to go to a party when she left here," Kara said. "But her mother has been calling all of her friends. No one at the party saw her. Not at the party itself, and not out on the streets before."

"Do we know if she went through the alley?" I asked.

"No," Kara said. "I mean, we don't know one way or the other. She left the apartment from here, not from her own place, and she was alone. But when I asked her mom which way she'd gone out, she'd looked at me like I was asking the most ludicrous question ever."

"That makes sense," Roarr said. "We know the adults never go that way, but don't know why they never go that way."

"If there's some sort of spell that drives them away, wouldn't you sense it?" Esja asked me.

"I would certainly hope so," I said. Not as satisfying an answer as I wanted to give, or as any of them wanted to hear.

"Everyone in the building is out looking for her," Kara said with a hitch to her voice. "Everyone loved Hailey. She's lived here since she was a baby. I think half the people who lived here have babysat her as a kid, and the other half have kids she babysat for."

"Right," I said. I had just finished tying my shoes and was on my feet. But before reaching for my art bag or any of my supplies inside, I headed to the kitchen and snatched up the bakery bag.

Chocolate croissants, just as I had surmised. And they smelled divine. They deserved to be savored slowly, crumb by crumb, preferably alongside a big mug of coffee. Alas, we didn't have that kind of time. But we still needed fuel to get moving. I opened the bag and started doling out the croissants, thrusting them into people's hands.

"Any appointments for you today?" I asked Kara as I gave her hers.

"No, not today," she said. "I'll be out with the others, looking for Hailey."

"I'll be with her," Thorge said, emerging fully dressed from the bedroom to take the next croissant out of my hands.

"Good," I said. "When did you know Hailey was missing? Before or after you went to the bakery?"

"After, of course," Kara said, her cheeks flushing.

"I only meant, you probably weren't looking for clues on your walk then," I said. Obviously, I hadn't meant she had heard someone was missing and *then* gone out for treats. "Can you retrace those steps, slower and more carefully? So far, as unlikely as the connection is, the bakery is our only lead."

"Besides the alley," Esja said.

"Well, the three of us are going to be checking the alley," I said, pushing one of the croissants into her hands.

"Again?" she asked. Then she took an absentminded bite of the food in her hands. Clearly she was doing what I had intended, just fueling up before a long day. But I could see when the taste hit her. Her face lit up, however briefly, and she gave the pastry in her hands a considering look before taking a second, slower bite.

"Are there other angles for you to draw from?" Roarr asked me. Not quite sarcastically.

"I think we'll be starting our work closer to the event this time than when Karen was taken," I said. "Or at least I hope so."

"I've texted Tlalli as well," Kara said. "She has classes this morning, but she'll be along to help this afternoon."

"Before her work shift, no doubt," I said. Wishing there was some way I could solve all this without her help. But I wasn't feeling particularly hopeful on that score.

We walked together down the back stairs and then along the corridor to the fire exit. Roarr slapped the door open and held it for the rest of us.

It was another gorgeous fall day outside, sunny with deeply blue skies. I couldn't smell gingerbread in the alley, but there was a scent of dry leaves I hadn't noticed before. I few were scattered in the corners of the alley, like there'd been some wind the night before.

But I had been sitting out in this alley the night before, and there hadn't been any wind.

"We were here all night," Roarr said, almost as if he were reading my mind. "We never saw Hailey."

"So maybe she wasn't here when she disappeared?" Kara said.

"Or she disappeared before we made it down the stairs," Esja said.

"I'll see what I can see," I said, settling back on the stoop with my fresh sketchbook. "If you learn anything at all while you're out looking, let me know," I said.

"Of course," Kara said. She consulted briefly with Thorge, then the two of them headed out of the alley in the direction of the bakery. Downwind from us.

I sniffed the air again, but the only smell that lingered now was the leaf smell. Dusty and dry. And perfectly normal for this time of year.

Esja sat beside me, and we both set to work drawing. At first the two of us were drawing in the same way, looking at the scene before us and capturing it on paper. Our techniques might differ, with me using charcoal and her using colored pencils, but our method was the same.

And we both tuned out the people who passed through the alley. This was a new occurrence, for sure. The only person any of us had ever encountered in the alley before was when I had met Gladys. But now it was like everyone from the apartment building was passing through.

The hunt for Hailey was breaking whatever spell or just mental block had kept them out of the space before. Not that any of them actually came towards us or the fire door. But they were passing from one end of the alley to the other, looking behind the dumpster or into the corners formed by the stonework that stood out like pillars from the brick walls.

After an hour of that yielded nothing, I was ready to give up.

"This is pointless," Esja said, tossing down her own colored pencil with a frustrated sound somewhere between a sigh and a growl.

"Maybe if you change positions?" Roarr offered.

"Or get some more caffeine," I said wistfully. I dropped my chin into my hand, ignoring the fact that this was a surefire way to get all the charcoal on my hands to spread across my entire face. I never could do art neatly. Not like Esja did.

It had been a while since anyone had passed through the alley, although Kara and Thorge had yet to come back. So the search must be ongoing, if no longer focused around the alley anymore.

They were probably expanding the grid, searching further and further out. And with less and less hope of finding Hailey.

Then something caught my eye—a flash of red across the alley from where I was sitting on the stoop—and just a little bit to my left. I frowned, then set my sketchbook and pencil aside. I stood up, feeling every ache of sleeping on a leaking air mattress compounded with far too much time spent sitting perfectly still on a concrete stoop, then stretched my back as best I could as I crossed the alley.

To find a very familiar hat half-buried in fallen leaves in one of the little corners formed by stony facade meeting brick wall. I reached down and picked it up.

As I had feared, it was Hailey's mushroom hat. Perfectly intact, the red bright as any Amanita muscaria, the white dots as clean as freshly fallen snow.

"She was here," Esja said, recognizing the hat in my hands the minute I turned around to show it to the two of them.

"That was not," Roarr said, pointing an accusing finger at the hat. "I would've seen it. I've been doing nothing but looking around, and I didn't see it."

"Lots of people have been searching this alley," Esja said. "No one saw it."

"Not even me, not until just now," I said. I reached out a hand, more tentative than I would like to admit. But all I touched was the rough, cold texture of bricks that had yet to feel the warmth of that day's sun.

"Where did it come from?" Roarr asked.

"That's the question, isn't it?" I sighed. My half-formed plan to go find something caffeinated was blown now. I put Hailey's hat in my art bag on top of my sketchbooks then looked around the alley with a sigh. "I need to draw again, but from a different angle."

Roarr just nodded, crossing his arms as he resumed his stance in front of the fire door. But Esja looked around with an artist's eye, hunting for the optimal angle.

"There," she said, and I nodded my agreement.

We both took up our supplies and moved to the very end of the alley. I was sitting just inside of the sidewalk of the passing street, but I was perfectly centered between the two buildings. From there, I had a view of the fire door and stoop, and of the dumpster beside it, and even of the area behind the dumpster.

I also had a view of the leaf-filled alcove where I had found the hat.

I turned to a fresh page in my sketchbook, set my charcoal pencil to the paper, and promptly lost all sense of time.

CHAPTER ELEVEN

THE SUN TRAVELLED across the sky behind me. I had a vague sense of that journey by the changing light on the open pages of the book I was drawing in. But other than that, I was aware of nothing outside of the marks I was making on page after page.

When I finally blinked and looked around with a normal person's awareness, it was like the opposite of when I'd awoken that morning. I knew that hours had passed, although it had felt like an instant. And I could remember things I had been drawing, the way on a more typical morning I would've remembered my dreams.

I dropped my charcoal pencil into the pocket on the side of my art bag and started turning back through the pages in my sketchbook.

"She's back," Esja said, and I realized she had been standing behind me, leaning against the brick wall as if protecting me from anyone passing by on the sidewalk. At her words, Roarr left his position on the stoop as if he'd been guarding the fire door for whatever reason and joined Esja in hovering over me.

I ignored them both, focusing all my attention on my own sketches. The first few pages were when I had been drawing just what my eyes had been seeing, before I had left the stoop. But then the perspective shifted, as did the technique, and I knew I was looking at what I had drawn in that fugue state.

I had drawn Karen stepping down from the stoop, half turned away as she put her keys into the pocket of her jacket. She had an empty canvas shopping bag and an overly-stuffed purse slung over her other shoulder, clearly on her way to the bakery. It was hard to tell with only half of her face in view, and that largely obscured by locks of wind-tossed hair, but I didn't think she looked like she thought she was in danger. She didn't look concerned at all. She was just an ordinary woman about to carry out an ordinary chore on a fine fall afternoon.

I kept turning pages.

I had also drawn Hailey, she too stepping down from the stoop. Her head was bent, so all I could see was the top of her mushroom hat, but it was definitely her. More than that, I didn't need to see her face to know she had been feeling incredibly anxious in the slice of her life my drawing had captured. Her body was rigidly stiff even in motion, her shoulders high and tight, her hands in tightly clenched fists at her sides.

She had been terrified, crossing that alley. But she had been in a hurry. And it was just a little distance to the road, barely more than a dozen long strides.

And I had told her it was safe.

I chewed at my lip, then turned to the next set of pages.

To find that the perspective had changed again, as if I had been sitting at the opposite corner of the alley, watching as the two of them crossed towards the position I was sitting in now and drawing their respective backs as they moved away from me.

"Did I get up and move?" I asked.

"No, you were here the entire time," Roarr said.

"You were freaking people out," Esja added. "Your eyes were vacant, but your hands were moving so fast. You looked like you were possessed or something. That's why I stopped my own drawing to sort of shield you from view. That, and the fact that nothing I was drawing seemed like it meant anything."

"Well, Ingrid is a volva as well as an artist," Roarr said. "You are—" He broke off awkwardly, and I didn't need to look back at him to know he was blushing furiously.

"Just an artist?" Esja finished for him dryly.

"I was going to say an artist and a valkyrie."

Esja didn't respond to that, but personally I thought that his was a pretty good answer.

Then something jumped out at me from my sketches. Just a little thing, but once I saw it, I couldn't unsee it. I started flipping back and forth more rapidly, comparing the different views. I had drawn Karen and Hailey both at least half a dozen times, from a variety of angles, although with sketchier details towards the end of the book.

"What is it?" Roarr asked.

"There's something going on in these sketches," I said, touching the charcoal gently with my fingertips. "Do you see this darker smudge?"

"Yeah, but charcoal smudges easily, right?" Esja said.

I looked down at my blackened right hand. And my right forearm, which I had dragged over many of these pages. Even my left hand had black on most of the fingertips.

But that wasn't what I was looking at.

"Smudges happen, but there's a pattern here that doesn't make sense," I said. "I draw with my right hand. The heel of my hand is surely what made these grayish smudges on the right-hand side of the pages."

I pointed to a few spots which demonstrated what I meant. I hadn't been resting my hand on the page, but I had still made contact with it more than once. If I hadn't been in a fugue state, I would've taken one of the blank sheets of paper from my bag and used it as a guard under my hand to prevent such incidental contact from smudging. But what I was creating at the moment wasn't meant to be finished art, so that didn't really matter.

Then I pointed to what I had noticed in the first place. "These are deliberate, dark smudges," I said. "Some of them are on the right and might be incidental, but a lot of them are on the left. I couldn't possibly have accidentally smudged those. Not this darkly, and with such stark borders."

"Also, they are always in the walls of the apartment building," Roarr noted. "Never the building on the other side of the alley."

"Oh," Esja said. "I see that now. So it's deliberate. Something about the apartment building. But what does it mean?"

I flipped back and forth, comparing sketches, but no features jumped out at me. Not even anything as open to interpretation as a hatch pattern that looked like a rune. Nothing.

"I don't know," I said with a defeated sigh. "Any ideas?"

Roarr and Esja both made negative-sounding little murmurs. But then another voice spoke up.

"Ghosts, maybe?" Tlalli said from where she was suddenly behind me as well, standing between Esja and Roarr.

"Ghosts? Of Hailey and Karen?" Esja asked, aghast.

"No," Tlalli and I said at once. Then we both blushed.

"Sorry, go on," Tlalli said.

"I think we're thinking the same thing," I said. Although there was no need for us to chorus it, so at Tlalli's nod, I went on. "Hailey and Karen aren't dead."

"You're sure?" Roarr asked. But he had no doubts from my tone, so asked instead, "How can you be sure?"

I shrugged my shoulders even as I pondered, but Tlalli said, "They don't feel gone, do they? I mean, not from the world of the living. They've clearly gone *somewhere*, and it wasn't just the bakery. But they're still around. Not dead. Definitely not haunting this alley."

"From when I've done this in the past, if someone died where I was sketching, I saw that," I said. "The body or the weapon or the crime itself. I saw something in my drawing. But all I'm seeing here is Karen and Hailey walking away."

"Walking farther and farther away," Esja said. "The last two sketches, they're practically in the street. And your point of perspective keeps retreating as well. Like you're going farther and farther towards the other end of the alley as you draw. Although, like I said, you never left this spot."

"But you think they're ghosts?" Roarr asked Tlalli.

Tlalli's face scrunched up in an exaggerated wince, head tipped to one side like she wanted to give a very waffly answer. But then she abruptly went straight in posture and serious in expression before saying," Look, like I've told Ingrid, I've never encountered a ghost that was like what they describe in ghost stories, okay? But I've crossed paths with apparitions that were like living memories. They look human, but they are really a human memory that—at least in my belief—belongs to the place itself."

"So the smudges in the drawings are the apartment's own ghost memories," Esja said.

"Maybe," Tlalli said.

"But you said they look human," Roarr pointed out. "What Ingrid drew are just smudges."

"Yes, but they are distinct," Tlalli said. I turned to look over my shoulder at her, joining Roarr and Esja in giving Tlalli blank stares.

She flushed. But she pressed on. "Look, there are three specific smudge images that keep recurring. One is bigger, but more diffuse. And two are darker with much more distinct borders, but always appear next to each other. They don't all appear on every page, and they move around in relation to each other, but there's always at least one big gray smudge or two darker smudges paired together. Do you see?"

"She's right," Roarr said even before I had started turning the pages to check. His memory was uncannily accurate.

"Three ghosts?" Esja said.

"I think you sensed them, but you didn't outright see them, which is why they are so very abstract in your sketches," Tlalli said.

"Do you sense them?" I asked her.

"No," she admitted. "But I've been talking to my mentor, Saoirse Duncan, about these things. This is a very busy time of the year for her right now, and she's doing some long-form magic she can't break away from. But she pointed me in the right direction to find out what I need to learn on my own, maybe get these memories to come out into the open. Depending on how strong they are, it's just possible they might answer our questions. At the very least, we'll get a better look at them."

"Do you think they are behind the disappearances?" I asked, looking at my sketches one last time.

Because I didn't get that sense at all. If they had been responsible, I feel like I would've drawn that much more clearly.

"No, I don't," Tlalli said, confirming my own feelings. "But they are there in all your drawings, I think, because they were witnesses."

"And we like to talk to witnesses," Roarr said as if that settled the matter.

"Of course," I agreed.

But there was one last impression I was getting from those smudges, now that I was perceiving them a little more clearly. They were, as Tlalli said, witnesses. They had watched, and they had waited. But they hadn't taken any kind of action.

But were they watching and not interfering because they couldn't, being merely living memories?

Or had they refused to interfere for their own reasons?

In short, were they friendly ghosts? Or something more sinister. And why had Gladys feared them so intensely?

Hopefully, if Tlalli's spell worked out, I would have those answers and more.

CHAPTER TWELVE

İғ I ʜᴀᴅ ᴇxᴘᴇᴄᴛᴇᴅ Roarr and Esja to object to being sent upstairs while Tlalli and I worked some magic in the back hallway of the apartment building's first floor, I wasn't exactly surprised when they conceded without a fight. The opportunity to eat a more substantial meal and maybe even catch a nap—two activities that had moved away from a want and closer to a need—was too good to pass up for either of them.

I did toy with the idea of asking Tlalli to wait at least long enough for me to do the same, but I abandoned it unsaid. I knew her time was a scarce resource, not to be wasted. And the more power I gained as a volva, the more I seemed to be able to use my magical reserves to keep mere physical needs at bay.

Although I'd likely be paying for it later.

But Tlalli, who had had a full night's sleep as well as a proper breakfast *and* lunch, looked like she had enough energy for both of us. Although why she was using it to sweep the decades' worth of dust from the hallway was beyond me. I watched her, half dozing, as she swept dust I hadn't even noticed from the light sconces, then brushed cobwebs down from the ceilings and walls before finally turning her attention to the floor itself.

"Is this necessary, or just symbolic, or…?" I trailed off, too tired to summon up more words. I had made the mistake of sitting down on the bottom step of the staircase and was fighting the urge to rest against the wall and let my eyes slip shut.

"A little of column A and a little of column B," Tlalli said as she put the broom back where she had found it in a janitor's closet under the stairs. Then she stood in the middle of the hallway and looked around.

But I could tell she wasn't seeing with just her eyes. She was perceiving through her magical senses. I tried to do the same, but as with every other time I'd tried it, nothing appeared.

"I don't see a particularly good spot to start," Tlalli said at last, then looked at me. I just shrugged, and she resumed her search of the unseen world around us.

"What are we looking for, specifically?" I asked.

"The veil," she said.

"So, is it *a* veil or *the* veil?" I asked.

She turned to throw me a questioning look over her shoulder.

"I'm confused," I admitted. "I think maybe this is more a Celtic thing than a Norse one, and I'm having trouble grasping it."

"But you have a veil around Villmark, to protect it from the outside world," she said.

"Sometimes we call it that, but it's really more of a protective barrier than… I don't know. Something resembling a veil in the conventional, clothing sense of the word."

"A veil is a barrier where it's possible for some people, sensitive people, to perceive something through it," she said. "Most people don't even know it's there."

"Okay," I said slowly. "But I thought the thinning of the veil this time of year was about the barrier between the living and the dead."

"That's the simplified version," she said.

"But we're not looking for ghosts in the sense of actual dead people lingering here among the living. We're looking to manifest the building's memories. Right?"

"Oh, I see what's tripping you up," Tlalli said. "The only barrier you've passed through is the one between Villmark and Runde, right?"

"So far as I know," I said with a shrug.

"Okay, so I have a bit more experience with this than you," she said.

"Because your mother and grandmother maintained a similar barrier over a hidden neighborhood in Mexico City," I said. A neighborhood that had become a lot more hidden when Tlalli was young. To the point where even she couldn't find it anymore, or discover what had happened to her mother and grandmother. I could only hope my gentle tone conveyed my regret at bringing up any feelings about that in this moment.

But Tlalli just nodded. "Yes, that. But also, I told you Saoirse, my mentor, has a fairy barrow."

"You *did* mention that," I said. "And I never asked any questions about it. I'm regretting that now."

"It's not like Villmark, or my neighborhood back home in Mexico," she said with a dismissive wave. "It's literally just a cave-like space under a grassy hill west of town. My mentor owns a hobby farm, so it's on her property. But she doesn't keep any animals or anything; it's just to protect that hill from outside interference."

"You said time didn't pass inside," I said.

"Well, it passes differently," she said. "It's slower there than it is here." Then she flushed a rosy shade of pink as she said, "It's how I can do things like keep up on my studying, mundane and magical both, and get a good night's sleep every night. With my schedule, neither of those things would be really possible."

"Handy," I said.

"Yeah," she said with a shy grin. But then, in the blink of an eye, she was all seriousness again. "Anyway, like I said, it's not like Villmark. It doesn't go back to Old Norway, or I guess Old Ireland, or anything like that. Saoirse is in Belfast right now, but she got there on an airline, same as anyone else."

"So the barrow has one kind of veil, and Villmark has another," I said. "But I'm guessing neither of them is like what we're looking for now?"

"No, this is different," she said. "Those veils protect sacred places.

They don't wax and wane, so this time of year doesn't make them any more penetrable than any other."

"Not like the veil between the living and the dead," I said.

"Yes, but *this* isn't *that* either," Tlalli said with great emphasis. "Neither of us is ready to mess with that level of magic. Not even to take a look around."

I felt a chill run up my spine, and I was suddenly sure that Tlalli knew this from experience. She had tried something. Something she had survived, but had been very ill-advised in attempting.

"No, *this* is a smaller sort of veil," she said. "It's the veil between us and all that the building remembers. And that, because it's so closely related to the world of the dead, does wax and wane. But we're not trying to see into the underworld. If anything, we're peeking into the otherworld."

"The otherworld," I said, but I knew this one. I had studied Norse mythology pretty heavily all through my teens and while I was in art school. But I had occasionally dipped my toe into other mythologies too. "Like where fairies and fae and that live."

"Exactly," Tlalli said with a grin. "Only, it's probably best if we don't draw their attention. Fairies are nuisances at best, and actual dangers most of the time."

"Sure," I said. "So how do we do any of this?"

Tlalli looked around the hallway one last time, then with a sigh she dug a piece of chalk out of her pocket. "I'm just going to cut a door and hope that that works," she told me even as she started drawing a large chalk circle on the wall, the one on the alley-side of the hall.

As she worked, I took out my sketchbook and examined my drawings. As best I could tell, the position she had chosen was the one where the smudges seemed to be, although the depth of field and perspective in my fugue state drawings wasn't what you'd call mathematically precise. Still, I silently approved of her choice of location.

Tlalli stepped back from her work to look it over, then moved forward again to make a few small adjustments, making sure places where the chalk had grown thin or skipped over the surface of the wall were as solid as she could make them. Then she put the chalk away and started the real work.

I couldn't see the magic weave she was handling, but I had watched her do this before. It was like her hands were unbraiding elaborate knots only she could see.

But if the veil had a weave, and the weave had a thinning place that had been darned back together, then Tlalli was most definitely undoing those darning stitches.

Then she suddenly said, "Oh!" and stepped back from the wall. Her hands were up in surprise, and her eyes were fixed on something I couldn't see but definitely wasn't the wall itself.

"What is it?" I asked in a whisper.

"It's an old man," she said. "You don't see him?"

I squinted my eyes to focus, then deliberately unfocused them, like I was trying to look at one of those pictures that has another hidden picture within it. But I only had a vague sense of a gray smudge off center inside her chalk circle. A gray smudge with diffuse edges.

"I see the gray smudge," I said.

"Yes, that's him," she said. "And now there are two girls here as well. Twins, I think. Although their clothes are so very old-fashioned. I mean, the man looks like he stepped out of *The Great Gatsby*, but these girls are like from the American Civil War."

I blinked. Two smaller, darker, more defined smudges were below and to the right of the gray smudge now, but that was all I could see.

"Do they see you?" I asked her.

"Definitely," she said with a smile, her eyes fixed on what I could not see.

"Do they hear you?" I asked.

"I think so," she said. Then, clearly to the apparitions before her, she said, "Can you hear me?" Then, a second later to me, "They say yes. They can."

"Ask them—" I started to say, but Tlalli held up a finger, clearly intently listening to something I couldn't hear.

I slumped back on the step I was sitting on, knowing I was only frustrated and impatient because I was really hungry and desperately needed sleep.

Then I felt something against my hand, warm and soft and oh so familiar.

"Mjolner," I said as he jumped up onto my lap. "Good of you to join us. I suppose you see everyone perfectly fine, don't you?"

He gave me a meow I took for complete agreement, then turned around and around on my lap before settling down into a tight tuck for optimal napping.

"I'm sorry if this is boring for you," I said, trying not to sound as annoyed as I felt. He might be a magical being with powers I barely understood. But he was also just a cat.

"Oh, no. It's a delight to speak to people who can actually hear us," a man's voice said, and I looked up in surprise to see three people standing between Tlalli and her circle on the wall.

They were exactly as she had described them. An old man with more age spots on his scalp than hair, but dressed nattily in a 1930s cream-colored summer suit and cornflower blue tie. He was looking at me, and there was a merry twinkle in his chocolate-brown eyes.

The two girls beside him initially struck me as more dour, but perhaps that was just the dresses they were wearing. They looked stiff and uncomfortable, buttoned all the way up the neck and with full skirts too cumbersome to play in. The fabric of their dresses was a dark shade of blue, but otherwise I had never seen two more Goth-looking girls in my life. They looked like a Charles Addams drawing come to life.

They both blinked at me with their inky black eyes but quickly returned their attention to Tlalli.

"I'm sorry," I said. "I interrupted."

"It's quite all right," the man said.

"It's good you can hear us now," Tlalli said. "I won't have to remember everything to tell you later. So far all we've covered is that they don't remember their own names."

"Alas," the old man said with a smile that implied that not remembering one's own name wasn't that big of a deal. "Miss Tlalli here was just asking us about your missing friends."

"You saw what happened to them?" I asked in a rush.

"Alas, no," he said with a sad shake of his head.

"We like Hailey," one of the twins said, completely deadpan.

"She's nice to all the children," the other twin said.

"Not everyone is," the first one said.

"Charlotte wasn't," the other said.

"I'm sorry, who's Charlotte?" I asked.

"Charlotte was their nurse, poor dears," the man said.

"Charlotte didn't believe us when we said we felt ill," the first twin said. "But we were. We weren't fibbing."

"No, I believe you," I said.

"Hailey always listens to the children," the second twin said.

"But you didn't see what happened to Hailey?" I asked.

"No, alas," the old man said. "We don't really see what happens in that alley. We saw her move through this space and go out that door, but she never came back."

"We tried to tell her not to go that way," the first twin said.

"We try to tell everybody that," the second twin said.

"But they never hear us," the first one ended sullenly.

"We try to just be very cross and frightening," the first one said, demonstrating her crossest expression.

"And sometimes some people can feel us doing it," the second said, clearly amused. But then she grew somber again. "But most people don't even know we're there."

"Not until now," the old man said with a smile for Tlalli.

Tlalli shot me a nervous look. "I promised them I'd be back to talk to them again. More of a chat and to hear all their stories." Then she looked at the man again, more directly. "But right now, time is short and people are missing."

"And we want to help; we just don't know anything," the man said, raising his hands in a gesture of defeat.

"Someone somewhere must know something," I said.

It was more an exercise in venting my frustrations, but to my surprise, the man answered me.

"You could always try talking to Gladys," he said blithely.

"Gladys? The woman who smells like gingerbread?" I asked.

"She always smells like gingerbread," the first twin said, and her sister nodded her silent agreement.

"Wait, you've smelled her?" I asked.

"Your suspicion is correct. Ghosts can't smell," the man said.

"I only meant, she was very clear to me that she never came in this hallway. I assumed she was avoiding you," I said.

"She feels us when we glower," the first girl said.

"But we can't make her go away entirely," the second one said.

I nodded, but then what the old man had actually said finally struck me. "How do you know what she smells like if you can't *smell* her?"

"She *always* smells of gingerbread," the first twin said, not quite rolling her eyes at me.

"She's always been here," her sister added.

"Always?" I asked.

"These girls died long before I even came to live here," the old man said. "They know of what they speak."

"You knew Gladys when you were still alive?" I asked.

"We didn't *know* her," the first twin said.

"We avoided her. All the children did," the second twin said.

"Not that she was mean or anything," the first one said. "But she was scary. And even then she was old. Exactly as old as she is now."

"And she always smelled like gingerbread," the second twin said.

"She touched me," I said. "I felt her. She had a physical body."

"Oh, she's no ghost," the old man said. "I don't know what she is, exactly. But she isn't like us. Quite the opposite, really. We're only here now because this is where we died. She's *still* here because she never has."

I was pretty sure my mouth was hanging open, but I couldn't quite summon the energy to close it again.

I was dumbfounded. There was no other word for it.

Whatever Gladys really was, she was definitely something I had never encountered before.

And I had no idea what to do next.

CHAPTER THIRTEEN

Tlalli had to get to work, so I thanked her, promised to keep her up to date with anything we found out, and tried not to feel too jealous about that fairy barrow she'd be heading to when her shift was done. Where she could sleep, eat, study, and repeat if she needed to before emerging once more with only a few hours passed in this world.

To be honest, she needed it more than I did. Still, having access to something like that would be nice on occasion.

But as I headed up the stairs with Mjolner close at my heels, I wondered if she was aging faster because of it. Like if she spent three days in there, but only one day passed here, how many times could you do that before you'd start looking older than, by the calendars of the outside world, you were?

Magic always had a downside. And the bigger the magic, the bigger the downside. My grandmother had created a wonderland where two worlds met. But because of it, she was very tied down to where she was in Runde. She could peek her head into Villmark from time to time. But I don't think she'd ever been more than a short walk away from her mead hall in decades. When she had taken a few months to recover the year before—a recovery necessitated by all that intensive magic over all those long years without reprieve—the mead hall had been closed the entire time.

And I thought it was a pretty good guess that Tlalli didn't think about her aging any more than my grandmother thought about just how much of her life force she was pouring into her mead hall.

Mostly, I was thinking I should bring it up with Tlalli at some point, just to be sure she was paying attention to it.

But there was a niggling voice in the back of my head that was wondering if I was accumulating a similar cost somehow. Something I wouldn't even realize until it was too late.

I didn't think so. But I definitely needed to find a quiet moment to take a more thorough magic inventory.

Despite the keys in my pocket, I knocked on the apartment door and waited for someone to open it for me. To my surprise, it was Jesús who stood back, holding the door open so I could come inside.

"You just missed your sister," I told him as I dropped my art bag in the most out of the way corner. Mjolner curled up beside it, as if to say he wasn't so much napping as guarding my not terribly precious art supplies.

"I heard her voice and yours from the top of the stairs," Jesús told me.

"Just the two of us?" I asked.

"Yeah, but there were gaps where it was like someone was talking that I couldn't hear. So I figured it was better not to interrupt," he said.

"We're about to eat," Kara said from where she was stirring something in a big cast-iron pot that dominated her little stove. "Are you hungry?"

"As good as that chocolate croissant was, it felt like that was a lifetime ago," I said. "Please, fill me up before Roarr, Esja and I have to hit the road."

"We're going back?" Roarr asked.

I looked from him to Esja, who was clearly trying to keep a poker face. And failing. She wanted very badly to be back in Villmark, even though we both knew the odds that her brother had returned while we were away were vanishingly small.

"I have to talk to Mormor, about something more involved than I want to handle in texts," I said.

"Get some coffee in her too," Jesús said, and Thorge nodded then went to get the coffeemaker going. "It's a long drive back," he said to me, like I was going to argue about the need for caffeine.

But then he grabbed my arm and drew me as much away from the others as was possible in that little apartment. He spoke so close to my ear I could feel the warmth of his breath on the side of my neck. "I'll be staying here tonight. In case you were worried."

"I wasn't worried," I said. But then I had to add, "But I do feel better, knowing you'll be here. Thanks."

"Don't mention it," he said. "This place is actually closer to the diner I'm working at now than where Tlalli and I are living. And I have a very early shift tomorrow."

"Did you learn anything? From what you and Tlalli did?" Kara asked as we all hunkered around the coffee table now covered in bowls of a thick, herby stew of beef and potatoes.

"Maybe," I hedged. Then I told them the whole story, about the old man and the twins, about Tlalli's promise to visit with them again, and about Gladys.

"So she's some kind of immortal?" Jesús asked as he sopped up the last of his stew with one of the biscuits Kara had made from scratch.

"How many kinds are there?" Roarr asked.

"Believe me, this is all new territory for me," I said. "The closest thing to a thought on the matter I have is that she has access to a place where time slows down."

"Like what happened to that boy Leifr," Roarr said.

"What's this now?" Jesús asked.

"Leifr is a Villmarker," I said, although with that name, that was probably a little obvious. "He was out in the woods when he was nine years old and went missing. When we found him again, he looked like he was about twenty. But we found him just last year, even though he'd been missing for a century and a half."

"Loke says there are places in the wilds to the west of Villmark where time moves at different speeds," Esja said. "Leifr was lost there for a very long time."

"He's being cared for outside of Villmark by our resident psychologist as well as Haraldr, my mentor in the runes," I told Jesús. "No one will ever know for sure, but Signi, the psychologist, is quite certain that he has more than twenty years' worth of memories, and more than a century and a half as well. She thought it was likely he had existed for more like a thousand years, if on a timeline no one else shares with him."

"How does that work?" Jesús asked with a frown. But before any of us could attempt an answer, he shrugged. "Time stuff. I've read enough science fiction to know how wobbly that gets. Maybe he was looping the same year over and over again or something."

"He's very incurious about it, but that's probably healthier for him than being driven to figure out what is unknowable. He's been getting along well. The last I've heard, anyway," I said.

"If Gladys has been here since those twins were here... the American Civil War, you said?" Jesús asked.

"Just based on their clothing," I answered him. "Tlalli might know more details about that than I do."

"Sure, but all I meant was, if this woman has been lurking around, getting a reputation for being a person to avoid crossing paths with since the 1880s or whatever, there *must* be stories," he said.

Roarr lifted his eyebrows as if impressed by this reasoning. "And you can find out about these stories?" he asked.

"I'm friendly with my local librarian," Jesús said in the tone of someone making a humble brag.

"That might help," I said. "If you have the time?"

"That's the thing with working the early shift," he said. "You're done for the day well before the library closes. I'll see what I can find out tomorrow afternoon."

"I can ask the neighbors," Kara said. "They avoid the alley, but if she wanders the streets outside of that alley, they might know her."

"Hailey knew her by name," I said. "At the very least, the kids might have their own hand-me-down stories to tell."

"I'll be sure to approach them too," Kara said.

Somehow, the six of us had demolished what had been an immense volume of hearty stew in a remarkably short frame of time. I split the last of the biscuits with Roarr while I finished the second enormous mug of coffee that Thorge had forced on me.

I knew we'd be making at least one restroom stop on the way home for sure, with that much liquid in my system. Probably more. But it was going to be dark before we got home, anyway. A few more minutes wouldn't change much.

"Give a hug to my sister and my mother for me," Kara said as she hugged me goodbye. "I text them all the time, but it's not the same as having them here."

"I will," I promised her. And wished I could promise my next trip to Duluth would involve bringing the two of them with me. But the more complicated our missing persons case got, the less likely it was I could safely promise to deliver on something so mundane.

It was a shame that Tlalli's fairy barrow was a contained space with no connection to anything else. It would be handy if there was a magic way to jump to it straight from Villmark. It would save me so much driving around.

But as I navigated my Volkswagen out of the spot on the street that had been spacious when I had parked there but was now tightly wedged between two over-sized pickup trucks, I had to admit my rusty driving skills were coming back to me quicker than I would've thought. I barely tapped the bumpers of the trucks boxing me in more than a couple of times. And only one of those was by accident.

Then I was heading north once more, the sun already gone from the sky but the moon not yet risen. And still a few days away from being not just full but being a supermoon.

And suddenly, for no reason I could pinpoint at all, I was sure that when that moon rose in a few days' time, all of this was going to be in the past. It would be solved, and the world would be right again. I didn't know why. I just knew it was going to be.

Everything was going to be resolved. Because the cycle of time was ending and beginning again, and we would get the reward for all the hard work we'd put in throughout the year. That was the promise of the rune Jera.

I looked over at Mjolner, who was riding home on Roarr's lap beside me. Mjolner was watching my face like he knew what I was thinking. I raised one eyebrow at him in silent question.

And he blinked back at me in silent answer.

Yes. He felt it too.

CHAPTER FOURTEEN

It was past ten o'clock when I had finally parked my Volkswagen at my grandmother's house and the three of us stumbled across the parking lot to the door of what looked on the outside to be a perfectly ordinary municipal hall, all lit up on a Saturday night.

But once we were inside the doorway, we were also inside the magic. Now what surrounded us was the thick timbers and thatched roof of a proper Viking longhouse. Despite the relative warmth of the evening, a fire was roaring in the stone fireplace that dominated one wall of the space. And the honey aroma of my grandmother's special mead was thick in the air.

I was exhausted, but the crowd already gathered in the hall was just getting started on their Saturday night. The noise of so many people laughing, shouting, and singing along to the music from the completely anachronistic jukebox was overwhelming.

But I still had work to do. I rubbed half-heartedly at my aching head, then turned to Roarr and Esja. "I need to talk to Mormor. Then I'm going up to bed. Thanks for coming with me to Duluth, and sorry we were there for an extra day."

"We wanted to come," Esja assured me as she gave me a tight hug. But there was no disguising the haste with which she herded Roarr past groups of Villmarkers and Rundians alike, ignoring their calls of greeting as she hustled him out the back door.

If Loke had returned, someone would've told us. Like Mjolner, who was still hanging close to my ankle. But I didn't blame her for wanting to be sure.

Or just wanting to be in the quiet of my house in town. But I would be joining her there soon enough.

I headed to the bar where my grandmother poured out mug after mug of the mead she brewed down in the cellar. She saw me approaching, and whether something showed on my face or if she was just concerned because I had stayed overnight in Duluth, she was clearly making her apologies to the people waiting their turn at her counter.

"Nora, I'll help out," my Rundian friend Michelle said, even as she slipped behind the counter to take my grandmother's place. Michelle was more than qualified to dole out drinks. She not only worked at the restaurant that sat just on the highway in Runde, she co-owned it with her mother. Pouring drinks, especially when no money was exchanged, was a piece of cake for her.

"Thanks, Michelle," I said to her, giving her the quickest of hugs as the waiting crowd immediately started hounding for her attention.

Villmarkers take their ale and mead consumption seriously. And any delay in their schedule on such matters was bound to be considered dire indeed.

Michelle just spared me a wink and said, "Kristofer is on the road now, anyway. And Andrew and Jessica are having dinner in Grand Marais tonight, trying out a new restaurant there. I'm the very picture of free."

Which meant I'd be delaying my bedtime at least a little bit, because there was no way I was going to leave Michelle all on her own. Her boyfriend, Kristofer, was a truck driver, and while that didn't involve quite as much time away as my own boyfriend Thorbjorn's constant patrolling duties, I knew the loneliness she was dealing with.

And we were all getting the sense that Andrew and Jessica, who had known each other for ages but only started dating a few months before, were probably going to be engaged before Christmas. As much as I had almost kind of, sort of started dating Andrew myself at one point, the prospect of this announcement coming any day now just made me miss Thorbjorn all the more.

And I had a good hunch that Michelle might be feeling the same way, missing Kristofer and trying not to be jealous of Jessica.

But for the moment, she was all smiles, laughing and joking with the Villmarkers with the aplomb of the most confident of servers.

Meanwhile, my grandmother had already retreated down the steps behind her counter, the ones that led to the rooms where she brewed and aged her mead. I had been down there before, more than once. But every time I came down those steps, I felt like a kid all over again. One being allowed, however briefly, into the world that normally only grownups got to see.

I was getting closer to thirty every day. At some point, it was going to click in my brain that I *was* a grownup. But it hadn't happened yet. And it definitely hadn't happened when it came to moving into my grandmother's special places.

"Kara texted me when you left her place," my grandmother said as she fussed over something on her worktable. "She's a good girl."

Wait, was that a rebuke? I was too tired to tell anymore.

"I didn't sleep last night," I said, hoping that answered whatever subtext I wasn't gleaning from my grandmother's words.

My grandmother just chuckled. "Tlalli's influence, I'm guessing. From her Celtic mentor. It *is* a big night for them. Not so much for us."

"No," I said, although whether I was agreeing with her point or not, I wasn't sure. "A girl went missing, and we didn't see it happen. So it was all a bit pointless, I guess."

"You can't expect to succeed all the time, no matter how careful you are," she said almost sternly. "Especially when you didn't have enough information to know how to prepare."

"I knew something was going on," I said.

"But not what that 'something' was," she said.

"I wouldn't have thought that going to Duluth would make me feel so out of my depth," I said with a sigh. "I haven't felt this at sea since my first days trying to be a volva."

"Well, nothing about what's going on in Duluth feels like a volva matter, so I suppose that's to be expected."

"Two people are missing. And I don't think what happened to them is the sort of thing that the police are going to be able to solve," I said. "The people who live there are doing all they can, but all they *can* do is just walk around and look."

"And that's not going to work because the two missing people simply aren't there," my grandmother said. Not a question.

"Yeah," I said. "Do you want to see my sketches?"

"I can take a look at them if you need me to, but I doubt I'll glean anything more than you know already," she said. "What came of it?"

"The sketches gave me the firm conviction that they are both missing, but not dead," I said. "And they also led Tlalli and me to talk to some ghosts inside the apartment building."

"Ghosts?" my grandmother said, half amused.

"Well, Tlalli says they're more like the memories of the building itself. Not the souls of the dead, but the building's fond memories of who they were when they were alive. Honestly, I don't know much about it."

"Memories of a place? I think you do," my grandmother mused. "And to know the difference between that and the unquiet dead? Well, girl, I don't think I need to remind you that you've faced the Wild Hunt."

"Faced in the sense of hiding inside of dead trees and keeping my eyes tightly closed," I said with a self-directed scoff.

"There's no other way to face them without joining them, now is there?" she said.

And, I supposed that was true.

"The ghosts or whatever told us about a woman," I said. "A woman who... well, haunts is probably the wrong word here. She *lurks* in the alley behind the apartment building. And she's been there since the current building was erected, maybe longer. She's been there since the two girls I spoke to were alive, back in the 1880s. And she's always looked to be the exact same age."

"Haunts is the wrong word because she's not a ghost?" my grandmother asked.

"She touched me the one time I met her," I said. "She was definitely real."

"Some ghosts can touch things," my grandmother said with a little wave. "Poltergeists can be quite overtly physical."

"You've dealt with ghosts before?" I asked.

"It was a long time ago," she said with another dismissive wave. "They aren't as common as most people think. But occasionally I have crossed paths with one."

"Okay," I said, rubbing at my forehead. "I definitely want to hear more about that when I've had a bit more sleep."

"If it were a ghost, you would've known," my grandmother said. "You would've sensed it. It takes a lot of power to maintain oneself as a discreet entity past death. A lot of power."

"This woman, Gladys," I said. "Even if she's not pulling down ghost levels of power, she must be doing something."

"Must she?" my grandmother asked.

"Well, she's been around forever and hasn't aged. So, yeah?" I said.

"Something magical is happening to her, but that doesn't mean she's magical herself," my grandmother said. "In fact, I'd say it's a good bet she isn't, since neither you nor Tlalli sensed anything magical about her."

"Tlalli hasn't met her," I said absentmindedly. "*I* definitely didn't feel anything. But if she's under the effect of magic, even if she isn't magical herself, wouldn't I have sensed that too? But all I got from her was the smell of gingerbread. Gingerbread on Halloween."

"Kids these days," my grandmother said, but I didn't laugh. In the realm of women who were far older than they appeared, my grandmother had never told me her precise age either.

"Do you know a witch named Gladys?" I asked her.

"Do you think we all know each other?" she asked with a smirk.

"Outside of Villmark, I don't even know how common witches are," I said.

My grandmother shrugged, not a helpful answer. But after a moment, she said, "There are two kinds of witches. Witches who grow up inside of communities like you and Tlalli before she lost her people. And witches who spring spontaneously out in the world. The latter have a very tough time figuring out who they are and what they can do. Mostly, they find their way to one of our communities."

"Mostly?" I repeated, incredulous. But something else was bugging me too. "And I've never found the 'there are two kinds of people' arguments entirely persuasive."

"It is reductive," my grandmother. "But it's true enough to be a useful framing tool. It sounds like your Gladys is a witch born outside of a community. And she never found a community."

I didn't know how this helped at all. Did it even explain why I couldn't sense magic from her? Because wild-born magic was so different from what I did that I couldn't even see it?

No, that didn't feel true. My gut didn't like it. I would've never learned a bit about my own magic without the help of my community, true enough. But the more I thought back on my childhood and teenage years, the more I felt little glimmers of memories that had a different context now.

Not that I was wielding magic with any intentionality. But a few things fell together a little too neatly to think nothing was going on.

And then there was the day that Mjolner turned up in my life. He was as purely magical as anything got.

"She never found a community, but I think the odds are good she found something," my grandmother went on.

"Like what?" I asked.

"Something like the fairy barrow, a place outside of time but not connected to other magical places. A nook, if you will," she said.

"But wouldn't I have sensed it, if it were there?" I asked.

She just looked at me evenly. Like she was waiting for me to come to some conclusion on my own.

And then it clicked. "We hide Villmark."

"Yes," she said.

"We hide the magic from the senses of others," I said. "But I can see it because I already know it's there?"

"Very basically," my grandmother said. "There are so many layers of wards on those protections. Like the wards that hide the mead hall. They are excellent at hiding things from the passive perception of even the strongest of witches."

"But?" I said. Because I could feel a "but" coming.

"Well, they are impossible to hide from a witch who knows what she's looking for."

"And what am I meant to be looking for?" I asked.

I wanted to say gingerbread. It was all I could think of.

But my grandmother just chuckled. "You really are tired."

"I am," I said. "Can you just tell me?"

"You aren't looking for the magic itself, whether it's a portal or a barrow or some other pocket place. That will remain hidden from you."

She made one last adjustment to whatever she was fussing with on her workbench and then turned back to me, wiping her hands on a towel. She was clearly ready to head back upstairs.

But just before she started up the stairs, she turned back to me to finally spell it all out.

"What you're looking for is the protective magic itself. Not the hidden magic. The wards that keep them hidden. Those, if you look hard enough, you can see."

"I guess I'm going back to Duluth then," I said wearily.

But not until after I'd had a decent night's sleep in my own soft bed.

CHAPTER FIFTEEN

I woke to the familiar sensation of Mjolner purring, his spine pressed against the back of my neck as he hogged most of my pillow. For once, not only did I feel completely refreshed by my dream-free sleep, I was up at a normal time and hadn't already lost half the morning.

As amazing as that was, the minute I opened my eyes, my day got all kinds of better.

"I was wondering how long it would take you to wake up," Thorbjorn teased from where he was lying beside me, head propped up on his hand as he watched my eyes flutter open.

"You could've just nudged me," I said.

"I wasn't in a hurry," he said.

Then he finally kissed me hello. That went on for a little while. But not as long as I would've liked.

"I have to go back to Duluth," I said with a sigh, and struggled to free myself from the twisting of my sheets and duvet.

"Yes, Roarr and Esja have been telling me all about it," he said. "Roarr made some sort of egg bake dish with sweet potatoes and sausage in it. It's better than it sounds."

"It sounds amazing," I said.

"Get dressed and you can have some before we go," he said, gesturing for me to hurry towards the bathroom.

"*We* go?" I repeated.

"Of course," he said. "Some nefarious thing is snatching women off the street. It doesn't have to be *my* street for me to care about that."

"I mean, it helps that it's the street where your soon-to-be niece or nephew lives," I said with a grin. Then I rushed through my morning ablutions.

The egg bake was just as savory as it had sounded and made a happy, warm glow in my belly. Which I appreciated even more the minute I stepped outside and realized that the autumn warmth had finally given way to an early November cold snap. I ducked back into my mudroom to add a hat and gloves to the fall jacket I was already wearing, then at the last minute snatched up a long green scarf as well.

It was a long walk to my car, after all.

As we walked, I filled Thorbjorn in on the parts of the story that Roarr and Esja didn't know, namely what I had discussed with my grandmother the night before. I had texted back and forth with Tlalli just before going to sleep, and while she didn't think she'd be able to make an appearance in the alley that day, she definitely would the next day for sure.

"So if I don't see anything, or maybe even if I do, we might be spending the night in Duluth," I said with a wince.

"That's not a problem for me," he assured me.

I wasn't a fan of sleeping bags and air mattresses, but I was even less a fan of complaining. Surely it would only be one more night.

Although I wished again there was a way to connect Tlalli's fairy barrow to Villmark somehow. It would cut hours off the trip, enough so that I could sneak home to my own bed at night even if I had to spend all day in Duluth.

But, alas, it was not to be.

On the drive to Duluth, I asked Thorbjorn how his last patrol had gone. And, as per usual, where another guy might've merely reported he had seen nothing of any import and even less of actual danger, that wasn't how Thorbjorn worked.

No, he—well, really, all five of the Valkissons—excelled at story-telling as an art form. And even the story of two days spent walking around not finding anything became a captivating tale of things he almost saw, things he could imagine happening, and all he was prepared to do in any possible worst-case scenario.

It made the drive feel blessedly short.

I parked my car in our usual spot and deliberately walked through the alley to the back door. But a casual glance around didn't show anything more than I had ever seen before.

Well, my grandmother did say I'd have to carefully search to find what I was looking for.

But I wanted to check in with Kara and Thorge first.

Thorge opened the door to let us in and hurried into the kitchen to put on a pot of coffee. Kara was lying on the couch with an arm over her eyes, but she gave no sign of being disturbed from a nap by our arrival. She just sat up and patted the couch beside her as an invitation.

"I was just resting my eyes for a minute," she told me at my concerned look as I sat beside her. "I was up early, talking with the neighbors and joining them in walking around the neighborhood. Nothing too strenuous, but I'm being extra cautious and taking breaks at appropriate times."

Her eyes were shooting daggers at Thorge's back, and despite the chipper quality of her voice, I knew she had only agreed to put her feet up for a minute under great protest.

"That's good to hear. We don't want you to overdo it," I said, perhaps a bit too loudly. Thorge scoffed but carried on with making the coffee.

"No sign of Karen and Hailey, I'm guessing," I said.

"No, not yet," Kara said.

"Did you ask about Gladys?" I asked.

"As indirectly as I could, yes," Kara said. But she was frowning now, as if thoughts were colliding in her head.

"What is it?" I asked.

"Just something weird in the way those conversations were going," she said. "The kids all know Gladys. I gather this is largely because Hailey has told them all to steer clear of her, although none of them knew why. But because Gladys just feels a bit off, I guess they didn't ask for a reason."

"That, plus they all really trust Hailey," I said.

"That's true," Kara said with a nod.

"The kids all know her, but the adults don't?" I guessed. "Is that what's weird?"

"Well, yes, it's true the adults don't know who I was talking about. But that's not the weird thing," Kara said.

"What's the weird thing?"

"Maybe it was just because I was asking so many questions," Kara said. "Maybe I haven't been as delicate or indirect as I thought."

"About what?" I pressed.

"The alley," she said.

"They've been using it. Walking through it while searching for Karen and Hailey. Is that what you mean?" I asked.

"No, more than that," Kara said. "They're starting to question things. Like why they had never used it before. It's like they suddenly realized they never did, but they can't say why they didn't. And it's really bothering some of them. Like there should be a reason they can name, only they can't."

"Something has changed," Thorbjorn said as he brought a mug of coffee over to me. I took it gratefully, although it was too hot to sip just yet. Not that that stopped Thorbjorn from taking a drink from his own mug.

"Like I said, maybe my asking things about the alley and about Gladys is what changed," Kara said. "*I* changed it."

"No, I don't think that's it," I said. "Something started changing *before*. People are going missing now. And I gather that's never happened before."

"I don't think so," Kara said.

"It's one of the things Jesús was going to check out while he was at the library," Thorge said.

As if summoned by the sound of his name, there was a knock at the door, and Thorge opened it to let Jesús inside.

There was a glow about him, and I found myself sitting forward at once. "You know something," I said.

"What?" he asked, genuinely confused. "No, not really."

"Then why are you grinning like that?" I asked.

Jesús still looked confused, but Thorge and Thorbjorn were both failing to hide their smiles.

"She's not wrong. You look very…" Thorge trailed off, looking to his brother for help.

"Up," was all Thorbjorn said.

"Up?" Jesús repeated. Then grinned again. "Yeah, I guess I feel a little 'up'."

"What happened at the library?" I asked. "I mean, you did go to the library after work. Right?"

"Absolutely," Jesús said, distracted for a moment as Thorge put a mug of hot coffee in his hands. He looked at it like he didn't quite know what it was, then took a sip and sighed in satisfaction.

I took a sip of my own now that it was cooler, and it *was* a good blend.

But I really wanted to know what had Jesús grinning like a fool.

"Okay," Jesús said after a second sip of coffee. "I have reams of printouts if you want to read all about it yourself." He dug into his backpack and pulled out a thick stack of paper, scanned pages from books and magazines from the looks of it.

"The gist?" I prompted.

"Duluth has many haunted places," he said, not quite putting air quotes on the word 'haunted,' but only because he was still holding that mug of coffee. "But none of them are in this area. And the alley behind this place in particular doesn't feature in any urban legends."

"If Gladys always looked like a normal human woman, if a slightly eccentric one, I don't think she'd be in any ghost stories," I said.

"I also checked crime reports all the way back to the founding of the city, or nearly," he said. "Missing persons cases. Theft and homicide reports. Just general news of the weird type stuff. There was nothing in any of the books or databases about this building or the alley behind it at all."

"It certainly looks like you were thorough," Thorbjorn said, nudging the stack of paper to fan out some of the pages.

"Yeah, my librarian friend went a little overboard," Jesús said. That grin was back.

"Your librarian friend took it on as a personal mission, it looks like," I said.

"So much so that she is going to the local historical society after her shift ends to see if they have anything that might be useful," Jesús said. "But she wasn't optimistic. Most of what they have, she has at least duplicates of. But you never know."

"I guess Gladys kept a pretty low profile," I said. "But if she's been here forever, scaring kids at the very least, why are people going missing just now? Why not before?"

"Maybe it isn't her doing," Thorbjorn suggested. "Have you seen her since the disappearances started?"

"No, I only met her the one time," I said.

"Perhaps she's not the culprit. Perhaps she was victim number one," Jesús said.

"Well, I don't like the sound of that at all," I said grumpily.

But Thorbjorn turned his attention back to Jesús. "When will you know if your librarian friend finds anything out?"

"And can you just tell us her name? Calling her your librarian friend is getting a little weird," Kara said.

Jesús grinned at her. "Her name is Olive, and I'm meeting her for dinner at seven."

"To go over what she finds at the historical society?" I asked.

"Sure," he said amiably. "Or it's a thank you for all her help. Or it's, I don't know, a first date?"

"I think it's that one," Kara said.

"Hopefully, the first of many," Thorge said, holding out his coffee mug in a toast. We all clinked mugs and drank down our coffee. It was a nice moment, enjoying a friend's milestone, as minor as it might be.

But with the coffee consumed, it was time for me to get to work. Karen had been gone for three days now, and Hailey for two.

And as little as I wanted to sleep on the apartment floor again, I really didn't want to watch those numbers keep ticking up higher.

CHAPTER SIXTEEN

I spent the entire afternoon in the alley again, combing over every inch of the ground and the walls. I even had Thorbjorn help me shove the dumpster to one side so I could examine the ground below it and the wall behind it.

I did discover some new smells. Just the usual aromas of accumulating garbage, but enough to make me grateful for the cooler air. I knew what heat did to garbage smells, especially from my days working in the diner in St. Paul, and I didn't need the aggravation of gagging while I searched. The fruitlessness of it all was aggravation enough.

But the majority of my efforts were focused on the little nook where I had found Hailey's mushroom hat. It felt like the most probable spot for something magical to have happened.

And yet, after hours of searching, I had to admit I wasn't coming up with anything remotely like a clue. Not even a hint of a lead that might show me the way to a clue. Nothing at all.

"It's going to be dark soon," Thorbjorn said.

"Tlalli will be here soon then," I said stubbornly, and carried on with running my fingertips over every single brick in the walls around that nook. I had been doing this a lot, and I had various scuffs and cuts on my precious fingertips to show for it. I wasn't going to be blending without tools for a while, that was for sure. Not with my skin slowly morphing into something with the texture of sandpaper.

"No one was taken yesterday or last night," Thorbjorn said. "That must be a good thing."

"I don't think that's because of any effort on my part," I said with a sigh. "Maybe the fact that it was Halloween really was important somehow. Now that it's a few days in the past, the danger is lessened. Until next year, anyway."

"No, if this happened every year, Jesús' research would've said so," Thorbjorn said.

I sighed. But I had to agree with him. Whatever was going on, even if it did somehow involve Halloween, wasn't an annual occurrence. Something had changed.

And I couldn't shake the feeling that what had changed was that I had made an appearance in this alley. No one had been taken until I had come to town.

"Nothing?" Tlalli said by way of greeting as she joined us.

"Not a thing," I admitted, straightening from my pointless task of examining the brickwork. "Is Saoirse back in town yet?"

"Not until after the full moon, I'm afraid," Tlalli said. "But I've had some thoughts about what we might be looking for."

"The concealing wards?" Thorbjorn asked.

"No, I'm talking about what the wards are concealing," Tlalli said. "To be fair, these are just random thoughts. Spitballing, if you will."

"I'm all ears," I said, folding my arms and leaning back against the stonework pillar.

"Right," Tlalli said, looking down at her own feet as she collected her thoughts. But then she looked up at me with a piercing gaze. "Are we really thinking Gladys is a witch like us?"

"Well, not like us, right?" I said. "I mean, my grandmother sort of implied she was a witch who doesn't know she's a witch. Although I admit I don't know what that means about what she can do, or if she can even do anything at all deliberately. I suppose it's possible magical things happen around her without her even knowing they should be under her control. Maybe she just thinks she's cursed or something."

"She feared the ghosts in the apartment building, you said," Thorbjorn put in. "I can't help wondering why."

"Me too," I said.

"Okay, but what we don't think is that Gladys has any tremendous power and control, like the women who you've told me about that live north of Villmark inside your pocket dimension," Tlalli said.

"No, *that* I would definitely be sensing," I said.

Which was a huge understatement. Those golden-haired women, troublemakers that they were, made no effort to hide their magic. It glowed like a beacon to my magical senses. Not missable even if I wasn't actively looking for it.

"So maybe this Gladys doesn't know she has power, or doesn't know how to control it even if she knows she has it," Tlalli said. "But what if she was drawn to magic that already existed? Older magic."

"Like what, for instance?" I asked.

"Well, like Saoirse's fairy barrow," Tlalli said. "I call it hers because it's on her property and she occupies it now, but she didn't create it. She found it. She sensed its presence and acquired the property that it sits on so that she could take charge of it, both for her own use, but also to keep it safe."

"Safe from being used for nefarious purposes?" Thorbjorn asked.

"That, but also safe from random people being drawn into it," Tlalli said. "Even nonmagical people are attracted to such things. It's why there's so many stories about people being lured underground by the fairies."

"So who did create the barrow then? I assume the fairies?" I asked.

"I've never seen a fairy," Tlalli said. "But I've never seen a troll either."

"We have," Thorbjorn and I said at once, then exchanged a grin.

"I know you have," Tlalli said. "But to carry on with my point, I don't remember much of the stories of my mother's people. I was so young when I lost her. But I do know the... I guess I'd call it the creation myth of our hidden neighborhood. It predates the Aztecs, you know. It predates the arrival of my mother's people as well. They were nomads who came to the Mexican Valley and settled on Lake Chalco and built a village there. But the pocket dimension was already there. They just built a city around it. And used it to hide from the Aztecs, and the conquistadores, and everything since in the modern world that they didn't trust. But it's always existed as part of the city. It still does, I feel that in my heart. I just can't find it anymore."

"If there were something like that right here," I said, pointing to the mundane pavement under my feet for emphasis, "Wouldn't we feel it? Like Saoirse sensed the barrow, or your people sensed the pocket dimension they moved into?"

"It's older magic," Tlalli said. "Maybe you and I aren't experienced enough to know what that *feels* like."

I pondered her point.

But Thorbjorn was already shaking his head. "No, Ingrid has sensed all sorts of old magics. She would know."

"I don't know if that's true," I hedged in a slow drawl.

"You sensed the ancestral fire," he said. "Not the one we all maintain behind the waterfall either. The true one. You touched that and felt Torfa herself."

"Yeah," I said, and shivered at a sudden chill that had nothing to do with the diminishing sunlight.

"Torfa," Tlalli said significantly.

"Yes," I agreed.

"What am I missing?" Thorbjorn asked.

"The ancestral fire was created by Torfa, but it's only a few centuries old. From the beginning of the settlement that became Vill-mark, yes. But what Tlalli is talking about is older than that. Far, far older," I told him.

"How much older?" Thorbjorn asked with a frown.

"I kind of think I mean things that predate humans entirely?" Tlalli said with a shrug. "I don't need to carbon date anything. I just mean we're looking for something that isn't going to look the way we think it's going to look."

"Like we're trying to look at chickens and find a dinosaur," I said.

Thorbjorn accepted this with a nod. But I was pretty sure he didn't completely understand it. Not that he didn't know what dinosaurs were. Villmark was flooded with too many books from the outside world for that to be remotely conceivable. He just was willing to take me at my word without probing my metaphor for possible weaknesses.

"So we need to change our approach. Somehow," Tlalli said.

I sensed frustration and desperation in equal amounts in her voice. But the depth of that feeling was a little too intense, a little too personal, for what we were doing.

Not that Tlalli didn't care about finding Karen and Hailey, and even Gladys too if she really was a victim and not a perpetrator.

But no, this was more than that. She wanted to figure this out, to find a way to sense what we needed to sense, not just so we could find our missing people here. But so she could take what she learned and make one more attempt at finding her mother's people.

I wanted to help her. I really did. But I had no idea where to even start.

Thorbjorn's mind, though, was still on something from earlier in our conversation.

"Torfa created the ancestral fire to protect us," he said. "But if what you're saying is true, she didn't create Villmark itself. I mean, our ancestors built the village itself, of course. And Torfa with her fire created the protections that helped hide us from outsiders. From whatever danger she felt might try to come all the way from Norway to find us. But she didn't create the world we live in. She couldn't have. It goes all the way to Old Norway."

"And other places," I added.

"It's a vast hidden world. And the barrier she erected only separates us from Runde," Thorbjorn said.

"You told me once that she left Norway because something was trying to wipe out her people, right?" Tlalli said.

"That's the story," I said. "Something about a new king and a battle lost, and whatever island our village was on back in Norway was no longer safe. So Torfa herded everyone onto boats, and once they were out of sight of land, she cast a spell to carry everyone to safety."

"But why Lake Superior?" Tlalli asked.

"It's very Norway-like?" I speculated with a shrug.

"But no one from her people had ever been here before," Tlalli said.

"Torfa brought our ancestors here about a hundred years before Leif Eriksson founded Vinland," Thorbjorn said. Then he frowned. "I have no idea how she knew to come here. We have sagas that tell the stories of various members of the first settlement population, but nothing that gives any kind of glimpse into the mind of Torfa. She just brought us here, and no one questioned it. The threat must have been very clear to everyone for that kind of blind acceptance of things."

"But how did she even know this place existed?" Tlalli persisted.

"She cast a spell to bring her people to safety, and this was where safety was," I said. "I admit, I never really thought through what that might actually mean. But maybe it does mean that she sensed Villmark. Even from across the globe, she sensed its power. And she brought all her people here."

"And then she cast her spells, to hide what she found from the senses of everyone else," Tlalli said.

"That actually makes a lot of sense," I said. "Villmark—I mean everything around Villmark, not just the village—is huge. And filled with things like trolls that don't exist anywhere else. But no one outside of the barrier even knows it's there."

And—I thought to myself but didn't say out loud—I knew we were still hiding from something. Something of immensely powerful magic. Something that was still hunting for us after more than a millennium.

"So what do we do with this knowledge?" Thorbjorn asked.

Which was a very good question. We had a sense now why nothing we were trying was working.

But meeting Tlalli's eyes, I knew she had no more idea than I did what else to try.

And it was getting fully dark now. Another day ticking by with no one yet found.

CHAPTER SEVENTEEN

THORBJORN WENT UP to Kara and Thorge's apartment to fetch food for the three of us, but Tlalli and I stayed in the alley.

Not that we were working on anything.

And not that we had agreed to take a break. We just stood there. Thinking.

"Maybe we should wait until after the full moon?" Tlalli suggested. "I mean, Thorbjorn is right. No one else is disappearing now. And we both kind of sense that everyone is okay, right? They're just not here. So maybe we should wait until Saoirse is back from Ireland. She found the barrow. Maybe she can find this."

"Yes, but the barrow wasn't hidden behind protective wards, was it?" I said. "The problem isn't just that we don't know how to sense this kind of ancient magic. From everything we just discussed, it sounds like that's pretty obvious when you come across it. No, the problem is the wards."

"Still, she might be better equipped than we are on that score too," Tlalli said.

No doubt she was. She had my grandmother's respect, which wasn't easily earned.

And yet, I didn't want to wait.

"Maybe we need to get into a more open state of mind," I said. "Meditating, getting more attuned to this place. Something like that?"

"You mean going into an altered state?" Tlalli said. She didn't quite wrinkle her nose, but I could tell she really didn't like my idea.

"I'm not talking about taking anything… medicinal," was the word I landed on. "I mean… well, like I said. Meditating or something."

"But you've already tried drawing here. So many times. Isn't that what you're doing when you draw?" she asked.

"Yeah," I had to admit.

"And you've been doing that repeatedly over the last few days," she said.

"Yes, but I only really went into a fugue state the one time," I said, more defensively than I would've liked.

"That led us to the ghosts," Tlalli conceded, clearly trying to make me feel better.

But I was in no mood to feel better. "And the ghosts led us nowhere," I grumbled. 'They weren't even proper witnesses."

"Not true," Tlalli said sternly. "We had no idea that Gladys wasn't just what she appeared to be until they told us that she's been unchanged for more than a century."

"Well," I said, then changed my mind and closed my mouth again.

"No, go on," Tlalli insisted.

"Well, Gladys felt off the one time I met her," I said. "And not just in the usual random street-person way."

"Because she wouldn't go inside the building?" Tlalli asked.

"Not just that," I said. "She smelled of gingerbread. That's the part my mind keeps coming back to. But it's not a helpful clue for me. I draw my way to answers, right? But how do I draw the smell of gingerbread?" I ended with a helpless shrug.

The heavy fire door banged open as Thorbjorn came back out into the alley, a heavy platter balanced on one hand. It was loaded with sandwiches, thick but cut into little squares.

Really awesome sandwiches, I saw when he drew close enough for me to make out details in the light from the single streetlamp that shone into the alley. The bread was fresh from the bakery, sourdough rye with flecks of caraway. And the filling was roasted chicken, still warm from Kara's oven, topped with generous dollops of horseradish.

Perhaps too generous, as that horseradish went straight to my nose at the very first bite, intense enough to leave me gasping.

"So good," I said before chowing down on a second bite.

"It really clears the head," Tlalli said with an amused gleam in her eye. "If I had any sinus issues, this would totally solve them."

"Maybe clearer heads are exactly what we need," I said, taking a second sandwich. They were the perfect size to fit in a hand. I carried it with me, munching in smaller bites as I made yet another circuit of the alley's darker corners.

"Clearer heads," Tlalli repeated, but in a voice filled with wonder.

"What are you thinking?" I asked her.

"I'm just thinking about what you were suggesting before, only maybe the opposite of that," she said. Then she shoved the last of her sandwich into her mouth and brushed off her hands.

I had to wait until she had finished chewing to ask, "What do you mean?"

"You wanted to focus extra hard, right?" she said. I opened my mouth to clarify, but closed it again at the wave of her hand. "Close enough to what you meant. But *I'm* thinking we should do the opposite of that."

"What's the opposite of that?" I asked. Because it sounded a lot like not trying at all. Which I wasn't going to be able to do.

"Maybe we just need to be open," Tlalli said, raising her hands out wide to illustrate her point. "Let the horseradish purge your mind of everything. Then look again."

"Well, I wouldn't say no to another of these sandwiches," I said.

"That one there has a touch more horseradish than the others," Thorbjorn said, turning the platter to offer it to me.

"It does?" I asked.

"I was saving it for myself, but if it helps the work..." He thrust the plate out towards me, and I took the sandwich.

"I don't know if it will, actually," I whispered to him.

Not that Tlalli was listening to me. No, she was standing in the middle of the alley now, head thrown back like she was admiring the stars, and arms wide open like she was trying to embrace the world.

Not that there were any stars to be seen. Not through the dense layer of clouds that blanketed all of Duluth at the moment.

I ate my sandwich, sniffling as the horseradish hit me with another wallop. Very pungent and sinus-clearing.

My mind, however, was as cluttered with worries as ever.

Tlalli, on the other hand, was moving again. She was doing something like a dance, but more random than that. And she was saying something I couldn't understand, in a language that wasn't English or Spanish. It was kind of a chant, but kept veering away from having any actual rhythm to it.

Her sort of stomping, sort of spinning, sort of sliding motion carried her across the alley, towards the nook where I had found the mushroom hat. I was just turning my head to tell Thorbjorn that what she was doing was an excellent way of avoiding the attention of sandworms when, in the blink of an eye, Tlalli just disappeared.

I heard the sound of Thorbjorn choking on his sandwich, and I knew it had nothing to do with the horseradish content. He had seen it too.

I ran to the nook, Thorbjorn setting the platter down on the stoop before following me. But there was no sign of Tlalli.

I ran my hands all over the bricks, just like I had so many times before, and found nothing.

"She was just here," I said. "She was just here and then she wasn't. Where did she go?"

I looked up into the cloudy sky, but I doubted that was the answer.

"I'm getting Thorge," Thorbjorn announced. "And I'll have Kara call Jesús."

I nodded absently, still scanning the leaf-strewn ground in the nook.

"Ingrid, do nothing until I get back," he said.

"I don't think that will be a challenge for me," I said drily. But at his look of concern, I added, "I'm fine. I'll wait. Go." I made shooing motions, and he finally retreated, scooping up the sandwich platter before heading into the apartment building.

And I was alone in the alley. The streetlamp overhead was flickering in that annoying way that streetlights do, and I could just make out the buzz from its bulb when no cars were passing by on either end of the alley. But that was all.

No, that wasn't all. I was smelling it again. Faintly, but it was there. Gingerbread.

Not that I had come up with any way to draw a smell yet. I licked at a bit of horseradish that had dripped onto my thumb and felt the bite of it at the back of my throat. But that was it. No mind-clearing revelation for me.

I dug into my art bag past Hailey's mushroom hate and my sketchbooks and found my wand. I let it rest loosely in my fingers as I held my hand at eye level. Then I bounced it up and down until it was a blur before my eyes.

Back when my senses were new and unreliable, this had helped me see the flow of magic around me. I hadn't needed to do this in ages. But maybe I needed the help now?

Only even with the help of my wand, I saw nothing. No portals, no remnants of the weave of spells, no wards.

I tucked my wand away again with a sigh just as the door burst open behind me once more.

It was Thorbjorn with Thorge hot on his heels. Then, trailing along behind, came Kara. She was wearing a jacket, hat and scarf and was carrying a pair of light gloves in one hand. I didn't have to ask what had happened; I could picture the scene.

Kara insisted she was coming too. Thorge came up with the only reason he could think of to convince her to stay behind. Although if he had tried making some connection between pregnant women and the dangers of catching a chill, I doubt it had been very convincing. But she had thwarted him, dressing up in more layers than any of the rest of us were sporting.

Although she was more sensibly dressed for the rapidly cooling night than the rest of us were. Not that I thought that was why she had an air of smug triumph about her.

"Jesús didn't answer, but I left him a text," Kara told me. "Thorbjorn said you were having trouble sensing what happened to Tlalli. Do you want me to try?"

"Tlalli said she was emptying her mind, doing the opposite of focusing," I said. "If that means more to you than it does to me, I'd love your help."

Kara just nodded gravely and then closed her eyes.

I did the same, but when that didn't help, I tried arhythmically dancing. Which was harder than I would've thought. After a lifetime of learning to move with the beat, I had to make too many conscious decisions not to fall into a pattern. Even with a lack of music, my mind wanted to tick like a metronome for me. And those decisions to ignore it were not really what Tlalli meant about a clear mind.

I quit trying, slumping against the wall with my arms folded in defeat.

I looked up at Kara, who was still standing just as she had been with her eyes closed. She had one hand raised ever so slightly, like she was using it to sense something. But when she felt me watching her, she opened her eyes and just shook her head.

"Nothing," she said.

"How does this fit with the pattern of disappearances?" Thorbjorn wondered. "I mean, if we're trying to find who's taking people, does this count as a taking? Or was it something else?"

"I think Tlalli did whatever happened to her just now," I said. "But beyond that, I don't know what it means. I just wished I had a way to get to her."

Then I heard a meow. A very familiar meow. I spun around to look at the stoop, but Mjolner wasn't there.

"It came from your left, I think," Thorge said, pointing towards the nook.

The completely empty nook. I squatted down and stirred through the leaf detritus, as if it were remotely possible it could be hiding an entire cat.

Then I heard it again, Mjolner's meow. Only this time I knew exactly where it was coming from.

It was coming from inside the brick wall itself.

As if he had been waiting for me to figure that out before revealing himself, Mjolner suddenly stepped out of the brick, his six-toed paws landing soundlessly on the pavement. He looked up at me, giving me a long chewing out in the form of irritated meows.

Then he turned and disappeared into the brick wall once more.

Only, just as the very tip of his gyrating black tail passed out of view, the brick itself lit up in traces of blue light.

And those traces of light formed a doorway. A child-sized doorway, but even Thorbjorn could fit through it if he bent himself double.

I looked back at the others, not sure if I wanted to ask them to go or ask them to stay. But Thorbjorn just gestured for me to hurry.

So I ducked my head, took a deep breath, and stepped into the brick wall.

CHAPTER EIGHTEEN

THE FIRST THING I noticed after passing through the portal was that I wasn't inside the building on the other side of the brick wall. I wasn't inside anywhere. I was standing in a forest of trees.

The second thing I noticed was that it wasn't nighttime where I was. I couldn't find the sun in the sky, mostly because the trees around me grew so densely packed together that the canopy was an interwoven mat of branches and leaves. Golden light streamed through gaps to fall in narrow beams down to the forest floor all around, but none of those gaps were large enough to show me even a glimpse of sky.

The third thing I noticed was that I definitely wasn't in Minnesota anymore.

And I wasn't in the woods around Villmark either. Those were mostly the same trees as in northern Minnesota, although the further north and west you went, the more the varieties shifted to more commonly Scandinavian trees. It was a subtle shift, but I had noticed it after Loke had pointed it out to me once.

But these trees were different. There were spruces that looked like those I was familiar with, but they were outnumbered by tall, straight coniferous trees that towered over me. Some kind of fir, I gathered from their needles and their cones, but I couldn't tell what kind.

Also, all the deciduous trees still had their leaves, and those leaves were an intense summer green. I saw oaks and beeches, which are common to the North Shore. But I also saw smaller trees that just had to be cherry trees, to judge by the barely faded blossoms scattered over the ground beneath them.

"Where are we?" Thorbjorn asked from where he was standing behind me.

"I don't know," I said. "I'm guessing nowhere you've ever seen in your travels?"

He slowly shook his head, but his attention was on those tall fir trees. They really were impressive. It was like standing in a cathedral where the pillars were actual living trees.

"Does anyone else feel like we're being watched?" Thorge asked, not quite whispering, but it was clear he was fighting the urge to do so.

We all murmured our assent, but Kara added, "Does anyone else feel like we're being watched *by the trees?*"

None of us said a word, but I knew it was only because none of us wanted to admit we felt just that. Not out loud.

The trees were probably listening to us too.

But I had a more important question to ask. And I directed it at Mjolner, who was sitting in front of me on a mat of fir needles, alternatively licking his paw and wiping his face.

"Where's Tlalli?"

Mjolner gave his paw a shake as he finished his bath. Then he turned to lead the way.

"Wait," Kara said. I looked back to see her groping around where two smaller trees grew, their tops bending towards each other and their branches interlaced. They formed an arch almost exactly the size of the child-scale doorway we had passed through.

Only, there was no doorway there now. The blue light from before was gone. And when Kara put her hand into it, nothing unusual happened. It didn't disappear here and appear in the alley back home.

She wiggled her fingers and then retracted her hand, looking down at it as if she were hoping it would feel something, like a tingle or a breeze or something. She straightened it out, then saw me watching her and shook her head.

"No way home then?" Thorge asked. He sounded more amused than put out.

"Not without Mjolner, I'm guessing," I said.

Mjolner meowed at the sound of his name, but that meow was clearly an admonishment to hurry up.

I started after my cat, Thorbjorn close at my side. Thorge and Kara trailed a few paces behind us, but not so far back I was worried about anyone getting lost. Despite the quick pace that Mjolner was dictating, we were all gawking at everything around us.

It was so quiet. I don't think I've ever been in a wood without a single woodpecker pecking, or sparrow chirping, or anything scuttling around in the undergrowth. It was just oppressively silent.

Maybe I could hear the trees breathing? Although that was likely my imagination.

Then suddenly Thorbjorn grasped my arm and pointed. I could just make out a mark in a bare patch of dried mud free of fallen leaves, needles, and blossoms.

"What is it?" I asked him.

"Sneaker print," he said. "Tlalli's sneaker print. She came this way."

"That mud is dry, though," I said. "That print looks old."

"It looks like it's been there for days," he agreed. But then he said, "But it's hers. I would stake my life on it."

"Another patch of forest that bends time," Thorge said. "Terrific."

"I have an appointment in the morning," Kara said. "Am I already missing it?"

"No," I said after a moment's thought. "At least, I don't think so. It's been ten minutes for us but days for Tlalli. So the distortion goes in the other direction."

"We can get lost in here for days, but only ten minutes will have passed outside?" Kara asked. "That's a relief."

"These things are seldom terribly consistent," Thorbjorn said.

"Also, I don't see a bit of edible anything in here," Thorge added. "That's probably why Tlalli didn't stay close to the door. She got hungry, and when no one came in after her, she carried on through this forest."

"To where?" I wondered. Because as much as we were all following Mjolner, Mjolner didn't seem to be following anything at all. There was no sign of a path, and while he was mostly going in a straight line, he was veering more to the right than the left when denser patches of forest forced him to divert. And he wasn't correcting afterwards.

But there was nothing for any of us to do except to continue following him.

It was hard to tell just how long we were walking. It felt like hours, like noon should've moved into late afternoon. And yet the angle of the sun—the sun I still couldn't see—never changed.

I don't know how long I was smelling gingerbread before I realized it. There was no breeze to carry the aroma to me; it was just like it was there, in the air, undisturbed until we passed through it. Then, like brushing through a bush laden with overripe berries, the smell was just released.

It was getting stronger by the minute. But it seemed to be everywhere, as much behind us as ahead of us.

"Wait," I said, pulling the others to a halt. They stopped at once, but I ignored all of their questioning looks, closing my eyes to focus all my faculties on the smell.

Which definitely was getting stronger. Even though we were no longer moving, and the air was too heavy and still to be carrying anything to us.

"I smell it too," Thorbjorn said at last.

"Gingerbread," Kara said with a nod.

But Thorge said, "Where's Mjolner?"

And I realized that when I had halted the others, Mjolner had kept moving through the trees.

"He was going this way," Thorbjorn said, leading the rest of us at a brisk walk that would've been an outright run if he'd been alone. I saw the furtive looks he was throwing back at Kara.

It was a good thing she wasn't noticing them. She'd have something to say about babying her, I knew. She had been winning foot races since she was five, and she wasn't going to concede her standing as the fastest sprinter in Villmark just because she happened to be a little pregnant.

Although I knew from what she'd told me after her OB/GYN appointment that running was on her list of activities it was recommended she not do. Because what she happened to be was a little *high-risk* pregnant.

"Can't you call him?" Thorge asked. I could see he was concerned about Kara keeping up even with Thorbjorn's modified pace.

"I can," I told him with an ironic grin. "But it never means he'll show up. He does his own thing. And he surely knows we're not behind him anymore."

"That he does," Thorbjorn said. "He'll be here if we need him."

"And if he's not here, it's because we don't need him," I added.

Thorge didn't look convinced, but he had far less experience with Mjolner's mercurial moods than either Thorbjorn or I did.

"This is just the kind of woods," Kara started to say, and I noticed she was ever so slightly winded. But she powered on all the same. "Just the kind of woods where fairy tale witches live. Right?"

"Like in the Brothers Grimm?" I said. But she was exactly right. Now that I was looking at it that way, I'd be willing to bet my life we were in some magically created—or magically partitioned off—part of the Black Forest of Germany. "I think you're right, Kara. That would certainly explain the gingerbread smell. Somewhere near here, there has to be a clearing. And in that clearing there'll be a house. And that house will be made of gingerbread."

Then, I promptly collided with Thorbjorn's broad back, crunching my nose into his spine.

"Why did you stop?" I asked him, rubbing at my nose.

"I have some tweaks to your theory," he said.

"Tweaks?" I asked.

"Well, it's not so much a clearing as an entire valley," he said. "And not so much a house as..."

Then he stepped to one side, pushing a few branches out of the way so the three of us behind him had an unobstructed view.

We were standing at the edge of a rocky ledge, steep but not dangerously so. We'd be able to pick our way down without resorting to climbing, although the steepness of the slope and the looseness of the scree were already shouting warnings at me.

But down that slope to the valley below was quite obviously the path we had to follow. Because at the lowest point of that valley filled with tall grasses and bursts of white and purple wildflowers was a palace easily the size of the one in Versailles in France. A palace with white walls with purple trim, echoing the colors of the meadow around it.

And the smell of gingerbread was thicker than ever.

Which didn't make sense. The walls were white. They looked like marble. With a trim of some sort of purple-colored marble. I thought that was a thing that the Romans had had? Purple marble?

At any rate, gingerbread was brown. I would allow for shades from light brown to dark brown depending on the molasses content or other variations to the recipe, but there was no way to spice it properly and still have it come out white.

And I knew from the smell it was spiced properly.

"Look," Thorbjorn said, pointing at something happening on the far right-hand side of the building. Figures the size of ants were moving around. Well, they were people, not ants, but they were so far away it was difficult to work out what they were doing.

But then it became clear. They were *building*. That wing of the palace was still under construction. And the people were moving from the scaffolding set up there, almost completely out of view from where we were standing, to rows of lumps that were emitting smoke.

Ovens. The lumps were ovens. And the people were putting things into the ovens and taking things out.

"I've made gingerbread in a loaf before," Kara said, her voice filled with quiet wonder. "It was more like bread when I made it that way, not like a cookie. But I suppose you could alter the recipe, make it even denser. Make it like a brick."

"Even if it were dense as a brick, would it be strong enough to build from? I mean, that place is huge," Thorge said.

Then I finally realized what I was looking at, and I laughed out loud. Thorge and Thorbjorn both shot me startled looks, and I waved an apology at them.

"Sorry. It's just, I think you can build just about anything if you're willing to use enough royal icing to hold it all together."

And if you caked the walls with that icing? Not only would it be incredibly strong, it would also be almost perfectly white.

Alas, no gumdrops or candy canes on this house. But I wouldn't be surprised if the purple trim I was looking at now had a lavender flavor, and the consistency of rock candy.

"All our answers must be down there, right?" I said.

"Right," Thorbjorn agreed.

And we started picking our way down the rocky hillside.

CHAPTER NINETEEN

I WAS PRETTY focused on my own feet and where I was putting them to avoid a nasty spill, so it wasn't until we had reached the scree-covered bottom of the slope and I was standing on level ground that I finally looked up and noticed the sky.

The thick canopy of the forest wasn't the only reason I hadn't been able to see blue sky or the sun. Now that I was standing at the edge of a grassland with the horizon clearly visible all around me, I realized that there *was* no sun. And no blue sky. Everything overhead was a whitish-gold haze. Like a fog that is just starting to burn off. There was light shining through it, but there was no brighter spot to point to and say, "That's it. That's where the sun is just about to appear."

But it was a haze that was high up in the sky. Everything down at ground level was fog-free and clearly visible. Although now that we were at the bottom of the valley, all I could see was grass. If I looked back up the rocky slope, I could just make out the tops of the trees at the very edge of the forest. But mostly I was looking at grass.

It was taller than it had looked from up above, taller even than Thorbjorn and Thorge's heads. But we had to get through it if we were going to reach the palace that was now out of sight behind the bobbing seed-heavy heads of grain and thick tangles of whatever kind of vine was sporting all the purple flowers.

Thorbjorn and Thorge took the lead, mashing down the grass as they walked so that Kara and I had an easier time as we trailed along behind. I kept an eye on Kara, but tried not to look like I was preparing to fuss over her. She had loosened her scarf, unzipped her jacket, and jammed her hat and gloves into her pockets. It was a lot warmer here, even under the foggy haze, than it was back in the autumn night we had left behind.

I shifted my art bag from my left to right shoulders to even up the inevitable neck strain that would be coming my way later. And tried not to notice that there was no sign of either Mjolner or Tlalli having passed this way before us. Mjolner might be anywhere in this world or a couple of adjacent ones, that I knew from past experience. But Tlalli *had* to be here. Somewhere.

I heard Thorbjorn and Thorge occasionally checking in with each other about what direction they wanted to be heading in. They were attempting to track by the smell of gingerbread. Which was indeed so strong I could barely smell the grass around me, although the green sap that oozed from the broken stalks where the brothers had stomped them down should've been filling my nose with its sharp vegetable aroma.

The problem was, the smell of gingerbread was so strong it was hard to pinpoint just where it was coming from. The entire valley was filled with it.

Then I saw a curl of smoke, barely visible against the haze of the sky, but I knew it meant we were getting close.

Thorbjorn and Thorge saw it too. Thorge made a sign to Thorbjorn, then sneaked ahead noiselessly, quickly disappearing into the green.

"Best to be unseen," Thorbjorn said to Kara and me. We both nodded, then followed behind him. It was harder going now, without a broken-in path to follow, and Kara was much better at being silent as she walked than I was. But I did okay, tired as I was.

I caught myself just before colliding with Thorbjorn's broad back for the second time and realized that Thorge had brought our party to a halt just at the edge of the grass. There was a sort of lawn starting just at his feet.

But this grass before us didn't look like someone had just mown the same kind of grass we were hiding in. No, this was a different, softer kind of grass altogether. It spread out like the green on a golf course, thick and lush all around the gingerbread palace itself.

And just in front of us, about half a football field away, were the brick ovens. They were squat and round with iron doors and smoke curling up out of their tops. I counted a dozen of them in two rows of six, but staggered in a zigzag rather than in pairs.

"Oh good. You're here," Tlalli said, suddenly at my elbow inside the cover of the tall grass. I bit back a yelp of alarm, and she looked chagrined. "Sorry. I got a little excited when I saw you through the grass. I feel like I haven't seen you in days."

"It's been about an hour for us," Kara said in a low voice, reminding us both to be quieter without quite saying so. "But from the state of the tracks we found from your shoes, we gather it's been longer for you."

"I guess," Tlalli said. "The light never changes, so it's really hard to say. I've been trying to figure out a way to get close enough to maybe get something to eat. But I don't want these people to see me. Although now that I'm not all alone, maybe it's time to just walk up there."

I dug into my art bag in desperate hope and found a battered protein bar jammed under all my sketchbooks. It was smashed, but still edible. I handed it to her, and she speedily tore into the wrapper and devoured the whole thing in two huge bites.

"I wish I'd thought to bring water," I said.

"There's a stream over that way," Tlalli said with a vague gesture off behind her. "That water hasn't made me sick yet, so I guess it's okay."

But then Kara said, "Karen!" Just that name, spoken softly but with urgency.

Tlalli and I both sneaked around to see past Thorbjorn and

Thorge, and indeed Kara's neighbor Karen was there, opening the metal door on the brick oven closest to us and peering inside before shutting the door once more and turning her attention to a child's wagon she had been pulling along behind her.

It was your standard kid's wagon with four wheels and red sides, but not the version that was ubiquitous these days. No, there was no plastic on this one, no thick tires that made the wagon almost untippable, nothing like a safety feature at all. Just four metal wheels and four brightly painted wood panels with sharp corners set on a plain wood frame. The handle she was pulling it with was also not plastic, but metal painted black.

The design might be old, but the colors were so new. Like someone had bought a brand new "not for kids" version at some nostalgia store for the purpose of home decor.

Karen was currently using it to carry bread pans stacked first one way and then the other, like bricks waiting to be used to build a wall. I couldn't tell across all that distance, but I was pretty sure the pans were filled with gingerbread waiting to be baked. They were stacked that way to keep the pans from slipping and getting dough on their bottom corners.

"What on earth is she doing?" Tlalli asked.

"Baking," Kara said simply.

Karen turned away from her wagon with a long wooden peel in her hand. She opened the oven door again and then started using the peel to slide several pans of baked gingerbread out of the oven and onto the end of the wagon that wasn't stacked with pans waiting to be baked. She repeated this motion a few times, then started loading up the peel with her unbaked pans to slide them in turn inside the oven.

"Why is she here, baking?" Thorge asked with a frown.

"She looks so happy," Kara said. And I had noticed that too. She looked like she might even be humming to herself as she worked.

What she did not look like was someone being held prisoner and forced to labor over hot ovens.

I tried to do the math, but quickly gave up. If Tlalli's hour had felt like days, what would Karen's days be feeling like? Months, maybe years?

And yet, she looked happy to be here, doing what she was doing.

"This has to be magic, right?" Tlalli said to me.

I blinked my eyes and shifted my focus. And yes indeed, everything around the palace was bathed in magic.

But not the entire valley. Which was odd. It was like this improbable place wasn't remotely magical. Only the palace itself, and the people gathered around it.

"We should talk to her," Thorbjorn said.

I nodded, gripped my art bag tight as if for support, then marched across the lawn to where Karen was just shutting the oven once more and looking down at the baked loaves stacked on her wagon with something like pride in her posture.

"Karen," I said as soon as I was close enough not to have to shout.

She looked up, startled, but then relaxed into a bright smile. "Oh, hello. Ingrid, wasn't it?"

"That's right," I said. "Karen, what are you doing here? Your husband has been worried about you."

"Michael?" she said with a little frown. Like she wasn't sure if that name was familiar, even though she had been the one to say it.

But then she was smiling again. "Why would he be worried? I've only been gone for a few minutes. I was just going to help Gladys with something for a bit. I still have plenty of time to get to the bakery before the lasagna is done."

I heard the sound of the Tlalli and the others drawing up behind me, and Karen's gaze passed over them all with growing confusion in her eyes.

Then she noticed the sky. And the palace of gingerbread and royal icing behind her.

"Where am I?" she asked. There was a groggy tone to her voice, like she was just waking up.

"You followed Gladys here," I told her.

"Gladys," she said, then turned to look at the front entrance to the palace. Namely, a pair of oversized doors in even more elaborate purple and white trim, currently closed.

Then she looked back at me like she was finally really seeing me, standing there before her. "Gladys wanted me to help her with something. I told Michael to watch the timer before I left, so the lasagna should still be fine. Although I still need to pick up that bread. But, wait. How long have I been here?"

"Three days," Kara told her. "Almost four now."

"Three days?" Karen said, alarmed.

But then it was like something washed over her, so much so she was swaying on her feet.

"Karen?" I said.

"I have to get it out of the oven," she said with sudden conviction.

"The lasagna?" I said.

She gave me a look like she wasn't even sure what that word meant. Then she bent to pick up the metal handle to pull the wagon.

"No, the gingerbread," she said. "We need so much more of it. I need to go set these out to cool and get the batch that's ready for the next oven."

I started to follow her, but Tlalli stopped me with a hand on my arm and a shake of her head.

"There's magic at work here," she told me.

"Obviously," I said. "But we can tackle her if we need to. Thorbjorn and Thorge can carry her home. Surely once she's back in Duluth, her head will sort itself out."

"I wouldn't want to bet on that," Tlalli said. "While you were talking to her, I was examining the knotwork of spells that was encompassing her. There were a lot of knots. More than I can undo all in one go. And with spells that affect the brain, just ripping people out of them is seldom a good idea."

"So we need to find what's causing this," I said. "So what do you think? I feel like the palace is a focal point, but I also feel like we should find Gladys first. If she's not the culprit, she's likely victim number one. Either way, I think we should start with her."

"Agreed," Tlalli said.

But Kara was pointing towards the far corner of the house, where the construction was underway. "As much as I'd love to find Gladys first, I don't see her. But I do see Hailey. She's standing right there."

I turned to see Hailey in a group of other kids about her age, although in her bright red dress with its gleaming white spots, she stood out from the others pretty starkly. They were standing at a heavy work table, the surface almost butcher block thick, each whisking away at something in a stainless steel bowl they held cradled in one arm. It was like they were all pretending to be housewives in some insane school play, just whisking and whisking as Hailey chatted at them and they listened.

I was just about to say something about her surely also being trapped inside the same spell as Karen. But then Hailey saw us gathered by the ovens and rose up on tiptoe as she waved at us enthusiastically.

"Not as much of a marionette as Karen then?" Tlalli said drily. "Because she's younger, or has been here for a shorter period of time?"

"Let's go talk to her and see what we can figure out," I said, and led the way past the ovens to the worktable.

CHAPTER TWENTY

Hailey might be wearing a mushroom dress with witchy tights and boots, but as we drew closer to her busily whisking group, I realized none of the other three teenagers were dressed exactly normally. They looked like they'd been scooped up off their bikes from some random Midwestern suburban street in the 1970s and dropped here to get to work making batch after batch of royal icing.

To be clear, they didn't look like three modern kids who had dressed like seventies kids for Halloween. No, that would've involved more bleeding-edge fashion choices. A little more disco or punk or whatever.

No, these kids were sporting bell-bottom jeans that were worn and faded, not stiffly new. Their button-up shirts were a little too clearly not made from natural fibers, the collars a bit too big and a lot too pointy, and that was quite aside from the garish color choices.

Which, again, weren't the kind of obvious, loud choices that someone would make for a seventies Halloween costume. They looked more like something a mother in the seventies had picked up at Sears or K-Mart. And, given that the oldest of them was maybe fourteen, they didn't have much choice but to wear them.

But the greens and oranges in particular were just awful shades.

Hailey, after waving us over, had gotten back to her vigorous whisking. But she smiled broadly as we approached.

"Don't mind my not stopping, but I'm so close to getting these egg whites stiff enough," she said, then blew up a breath that briefly lifted her bangs off her forehead.

"Who are your new friends?" I asked her. "Are they from the neighborhood?"

"No, I just met them here," Hailey said, then pointed with her chin first at the oldest, spotty-faced boy with hair buzzed so short I couldn't quite guess the color, then a girl with perfectly feathered wings of blond hair framing her face, and then a boy of about twelve with dark red hair in a scruffy shag haircut. "This is David MacKay and Kimberly and Mark Sutton."

Each of the kids returned my quick waves of hello with blank stares before returning their attention to their respective bowls of icing.

"Sugar crash?" I said. Although none of them seemed to be sampling the goods.

"They're just shy," Hailey said. But she sounded like their reaction had confused her too.

"How long have they been here?" I asked. Not that I really thought she'd say "fifty years" out loud or anything. But Hailey just shrugged and carried on beating her egg whites.

Which would be so much easier to do with a mixer, but clearly there was nowhere here to plug such a thing in.

"Hailey, you know people have been looking for you," Kara said.

Hailey gave her a puzzled look. "From the party? I mean, I know I was running late, but I've only been here for a few minutes. I doubt anyone there has even noticed I'm not there yet. I mean, it's a *party*. Who takes attendance?"

"It's November second," Kara told her. "And despite the light here, it's actually the middle of the night."

"Or it was, when we left," Thorge said in a low rumble.

"That doesn't make any sense," Hailey said, in a voice that implied she would, ergo, disregard what Kara said completely.

She lifted her whisk out of her bowl to check the consistency of her egg whites, then found the soft peaks unacceptable and returned to the work of whisking.

"I have something for you," I said, digging into my art bag. I had stuffed her hat in there after I found it, and the cardboard frame was bent, but it was still recognizable. I straightened it out as best I could and then held it out for her.

Wonder of wonders, she stopped whisking to reach for the hat. She touched it, at first as if she wasn't even sure what it was, but then with an air of nostalgia. Like I had waited to hand her the same hat at her fiftieth birthday or something, some distant memory she had forgotten she had even remembered.

"It matches my dress," she said. She put it on her head, but the bent cardboard gave it a crazy tilt, blocking half her vision. She tried adjusting it, but gently so as not to ruin the folds of the cheesecloth.

"Hailey," the boy she had called David said. Just her name, briefly spoken, and he didn't even look up at her when he did it. But something about hearing her name spoken that way ruined the effect of seeing her hat again. She promptly took it off, dropped it on the grass behind her, then got back to work whisking.

"David," I said, moving around the table until I was standing right next to him. But not on his whisking arm side. I had a feeling that interfering with his mixing was likely to provoke violence.

He didn't look up at me, but I felt like he was listening to me all the same. People's names are powerful things. Sometimes hearing it is all it takes to break a spell, or at least weaken it enough for the victim to escape on their own.

Not in this case, though. He carried on mixing the icing for all he was worth.

"David," I said again. "How long have you been here? Are your parents looking for you?"

"No," he said numbly. "They don't get home from work for hours yet. No one is looking for us."

"Are you sure?" I pressed. "Because Hailey doesn't think so either, and yet we're all here because we *were* looking for her. And her mother is very worried about her."

David grunted, but nothing even resembling a word was contained in that grunt.

"Do we try tackling them and carrying them out of here?" Thorbjorn asked.

"No, I agree with Tlalli that it would be a bad idea," Kara said. "I don't think they'd take it well. And I'm worried if we try doing that without breaking the spell first, it might break something else. Like their minds."

"Maybe," I said, not wanting to play the worst-case scenario game just yet. "It's better not to risk it until we know more, but I don't think they're in active danger. They look well-fed and unharmed. Although the forced labor is bothersome."

"To say the least," Thorge said.

"If you don't think it would hurt them to try, why not risk breaking them out of here?" Thorbjorn asked.

Then I realized there was a part of what was going on here that my Villmarker friends weren't grasping. And Tlalli had wandered away, strolling past the tables of cooling gingerbread bricks to watch the people moving around on the scaffolding, laying the bricks and cementing them all together with the royal icing.

I pulled at Thorbjorn's sleeve, waving for Thorge and Kara to also follow as I dragged him just out of earshot of the whisking teenagers.

"What is it?" Thorbjorn asked.

"Those kids. They don't belong here," I said. Then I shook my head at my own word choices before anyone else could say a thing. "No, obviously, no one *belongs* here. I'm saying, even if we could pull them back out of the portal with us, back to where we left, we could get Hailey and Karen home, but not these others. They don't belong there either. Not in 2025. No, I think as much as they only think they've been here for a few minutes, the same as Hailey and Karen do, they've been here since 1975, maybe a little longer."

"But Jesús searched for missing persons cases in the neighborhood, and there weren't any," Kara said. "He went back a lot longer than 1975 too."

"Which is good," Tlalli said as she rejoined us. "Because some of these people go back a lot longer than that too."

"You noticed what I did about their clothes," I said. Not a question.

"Yes, but you should take a look at the adults working the walls. Their clothing choices are even more antiquated," she said. But she didn't sound like she was trying for a joke at all.

"Something worse is bothering you," I guessed.

"Some of them are wearing tatters of old-fashioned clothes," she said. "I see Edwardian, Victorian, and even what has to be from the Middle Ages. And some of them don't fit right. I mean, they're not just worn out from being the only outfit they've been wearing for who knows how long. No, their bodies have grown out of them. They're clearly middle-aged adults wearing children's clothes. Faded and torn at the seams and very, very filthy."

"Everyone here was taken as a child?" I asked, horrified.

"Well, Karen," Kara said.

"And like I said, it's not everyone. I'd say about half of the people I just saw," Tlalli said.

"Right, but still. Gingerbread house and lots of missing children. It kind of fits," I said.

"We've seen the gingerbread house and the children," Thorbjorn said. "So where's the witch?"

"And how is she maintaining the level of spells in Duluth she'd need to be weaving to make sure no one knows these kids are missing for years and years?" Tlalli asked.

"And why didn't she do it with Hailey and Karen?" I added. "Because it doesn't make sense."

"None of it makes any sense," Kara said. "I mean, in the story, the witch built the gingerbread house to lure in children so she could eat them, right?"

"She made the girl do chores," Thorbjorn said.

"So this gingerbread witch is making all of them do chores, I guess," I said.

"But if the only chore is expanding the gingerbread house to palatial proportions, what's the point of it all?" Tlalli asked. "Why would you kidnap people to help you perfect the trap you use to kidnap people? It's all so circular."

"I kind of want to take a look around inside the house," I said, but made no move towards the front entrance.

Because the only reason I wasn't arguing against anything Tlalli was saying was that I was afraid of the possible answer.

If the witch was using the gingerbread house to lure in kids to eat, then the fact that she was luring in extra kids to expand her trap *did* make sense. But only if the number of children she was eating was so much more than the dozen or so adults, children and former children we saw around us, building the new wing on her house.

The inside of that palace might be one big charnel house. And I wasn't in a hurry to see that with my own eyes.

But then, even as I looked at those immense double doors and shifted nervously in the throes of my attempts at decision-making, one of the doors opened. Not fully, just wide enough to let a single figure slip outside.

It was Gladys.

She was already striding across the lawn to approach Hailey and the other three teenagers and didn't seem to have noticed the five of us standing halfway to the grass line. Halfway to safety, if we wanted to make a run for it.

Only, I wasn't getting powerful witch vibes off Gladys at all. The palace behind her was still glowing with the power of *somebody's* spells. But she seemed to be perfectly ordinary. Just like all the others working on the construction project.

Although clearly they weren't. They were all stumbling around like zombies. At least, all save for Hailey and Karen, who were so intensely focused on their tasks that someone might be inclined to compare them to zombies. Until they were standing side by side with actual zombies, that is. Looking from Karen pulling her wagon towards another of the brick ovens and the woman standing vacantly at the table where Karen had just arrayed her latest haul of baked gingerbread, the difference between the two wasn't hard to spot.

But I was sure that, given enough time, Karen would become more and more like the others. And so would Hailey.

And yet Gladys, who by everything I knew would've been here longer than anybody, seemed unaffected.

I mean, she was clearly *off*. But she wasn't a zombie.

"We need to talk to Gladys," I said at last.

Thorbjorn nodded and then led the way back to the icing table.

CHAPTER TWENTY-ONE

GLADYS WAS NO LONGER WEARING her wool coat, a coat I couldn't quite recall clearly enough to date it from memory now. I had assumed when I had seen it the first time that it had been a hand-me-down from a husband or brother or possibly even a father, or that she had picked it up from a thrift store. I had, in short, assumed it was old. But now I was really curious about just how old it was.

Alas, what she was wearing now was a pair of gray sweatpants, orthopedic sneakers that were modern but also just about worn out—more gray than white now with laces that hung in limp bows—and a pink T-shirt with a picture of a Japanese cat character, possibly from some anime I didn't know.

As little as I knew about Gladys, that didn't feel like her style. More like something she'd picked up somewhere and only worn because clothes had a function and this item served that function as well as any other.

So modern, but not new. Which still didn't mean that Gladys was exactly as old as she looked like she was. Given where she spent most of her time, I found it very unlikely she had been born anywhere near the 1940s or 1950s.

Her age would've been hard to guess without time portals

involved, though. Like I had noticed before, she moved with the grace and strength of someone in their prime. The fact that her hair was steel gray with no hint of the color of her younger days left didn't tell me much. Some people started going gray in high school, after all.

But her skin was very deeply lined, and she had age spots everywhere. Her hands might grip with the strength of a gymnast ready to do a rings routine, but her skin had that crepey, easily torn look.

The one thing that was indisputable, though, was that as strong as she may be, she packed that strength into a very petite frame. As she stood at the icing table saying something to Hailey and the three teenagers, even Mark, who looked all of twelve, towered over her.

I thought she was instructing them in their work or something, but my blood chilled when I heard what she was actually saying to Hailey.

"Dear, you must have friends who'd also like to help?" she said in a pleading sort of voice. Like she wanted to sound more helpless than she actually was.

David, Mark and Kimberly were still whisking egg whites. But Hailey looked up, initially to answer Gladys, but when I and my friends with me drew up close behind Gladys, Hailey's eyes shifted to mine.

And Gladys turned to see what had drawn Hailey's attention away. Her face flushed at once, a deep crimson as her eyes dropped away from mine. That was a flush of shame, I just knew it.

"Gladys," I said. "We met before, although we weren't properly introduced. Do you remember?"

"I get confused," she mumbled, still not looking at me.

"If what's going on here is anything like what I'm imagining, I can certainly see why that would be true," I said with as much gentleness as I could muster. But I wasn't going to let her get away with not explaining things to me. "But you do remember me."

"Yes," she said grudgingly.

"You helped me with the door, to get into the apartment building," I said, and her eyes shot up to mine with a sudden glow of recognition. It was just possible she wasn't pretending to be confused. But she definitely remembered me now. "You helped me then, and I'm here to help you now."

"Oh. Wonderful," Gladys said. She turned and started to point to the scaffolding on the new wing of her palace.

But I spoke again before she could even start with whatever she was going to say next. "Not with building this house, Gladys. I think you know all this has to go."

"It's not mine," Gladys said.

For an instant, I thought she was just trying to duck blame. But the nervous glance she shot my way said something else.

She was scared.

"Whose is it?" I asked.

"I've forgotten her name. Truly," Gladys said earnestly, all but wringing her hands together in her dismay. "She left when I was young. I don't know how young," she added forcefully, with raw frustration. "And I don't know how long ago. Everything here is loopy and confusing."

"Do you remember where you're from?" Kara asked her. "Before all this happened? You must've been living somewhere out in the world before you were taken and brought here, right?"

Gladys nodded mutely but didn't answer.

"Can you remember anything at all?" I asked her.

She chewed at her lip, her eyes unfocused for a moment. Then she said, "I lived in a house by a lake. A lake so huge you couldn't see the other side of it. My father went out every morning to fish, and my mother helped him clean all the fish when he came back at the end of the day. I sat by the fire, and I watched my brother. He was just a baby, but I was a good sister. I took care of him."

"But then you ended up here," I said.

"I don't remember how," Gladys said. "Sometimes I think I've always been here. It feels like I have. But then I remember rocking my brother in his cradle by the fire and the smell of fish everywhere. It's not even a memory, really. It's like I remember a picture from a book that I think I've read, only all I remember is the picture. Not the story. But he was my brother. I know he was."

"It's possible you'd be able to remember more," I told her. "I know people who can help you try, anyway."

"I can't leave here," Gladys said at once. "It's impossible. Quite impossible."

"But you leave here all the time," Kara said. "People have seen you in Duluth for more than a hundred years."

"I can go, but I have to come back," Gladys said. "I don't understand how anything works out there, but I understand things here. The stove makes food when I'm hungry, and the well always has water. As long as I maintain the house, it will keep me warm and safe forever."

"So why do you leave it at all?" I asked her. "Why do you go up to the forest and step through the portals in the trees?"

"Well," she said, blinking back tears now. "I think I have to? I'm supposed to? The woman I can't quite remember, she used to make me go. Because the house needed more work done than the two of us could do. But she couldn't leave at all. So she pushed me out through the portals and wouldn't let me come back without more help for her. She's been gone for ages and ages. I don't know where. I just came back one time and she was gone. But she might come back. Any day now, she might come back. So I keep doing all the tasks she set for me. Including going out there to find helpers. But I hate it out there, it's so confusing."

"Because it's noisy and smelly and covered in brick and concrete?" Kara asked.

I shot her a look, a bit worried that this was her impression of Duluth. That she didn't like it there. But she gave me the smallest shake of her head. No, she was just trying to find a common bond with Gladys.

But Gladys was also shaking her head. "No, you don't understand."

"Please explain, then," I said.

"I can go out through portals, yes, but I don't get to pick which ones," she said. "The woman used to open them for me, but that's gone now and I can't do what she did. When I need more help, I have to sit on the ground and wait for something to open. Sometimes it takes days. Or longer, I can't even…" She broke off with a vague gesture to the sky, but I understood her. Talking about time here was never going to be very precise.

But I just nodded for her to go on with her story.

"The portals, when they open, I never know where they're going to go," she said. "You think I'd memorize every portal's location here and where it takes me there, or mark the trees, or something. But it's always changing. I can't know anything. I just see the blue light and run through it."

"And then you're in the alley behind the apartment building?" I asked.

"Sometimes," she said grudgingly. "Sometimes it's different because the buildings are different. Sometimes there's nothing there but a grassy hillside. And sometimes it's all wooden shanties and smoke from coal fires. I never know where I'm going until I get there."

"But once you get there, you find someone to follow you back here. Right?" I asked.

Gladys flushed that guilty shade of red again. But she sounded like a sullen toddler when she said, "I had to. She made me."

"But she's been gone for a very long time," I said. "And yet you keep taking people."

"I have to," she insisted. I felt like she wanted to kick at the ground but was just managing to fight the impulse.

"Why would you do to others what was done to you?" Kara asked her. "You're taking them from families too. From their own baby brothers, and parents, and everyone."

"And you must see what's happening to them," I added. "Whatever that woman did that kept you yourself here, it's clearly not working for the others. They're losing themselves, all their memories and personality and everything. What do you do with them when they're all used up?"

"No one is all used up," she said, her blue eyes boring angrily into mine. "I take care of everyone. Everyone! No one ever has to leave."

"Everyone you've ever taken is still here?" Tlalli said even as she craned her head like she was doing a quick count of all the people she could see.

"Everyone," Gladys said. "I make sure everyone eats and everyone has a bed to sleep in. It's not my fault that they get all dull and stupid and stop talking to me."

"So whose fault is it, then?" Thorbjorn asked in a mild voice. "The house? Is the house itself consuming them?"

"It's just a house," Gladys said. But she wasn't making eye contact with any of us again, so I was pretty sure she at least had a suspicion that wasn't entirely true.

"You don't remember where you came from," I said at last. "Do you remember where the others came from?"

"Not really," she said. "Some of them, kind of. But I told you, I can't make the portals go anywhere. They take me where they want to. Even if I knew where everyone belonged, I couldn't put them back. So I keep them here. And I take care of them."

"Some of them clearly need some new clothes," Tlalli mumbled, but I gestured for her to keep it quiet. Not that it wasn't true. But in this moment, it wasn't helpful.

"Gladys, all of this is beyond me," I admitted.

Gladys grunted a response.

"But I think I know someone who can help," I said.

"I doubt it," she said, the sullen toddler once more.

"The first thing we have to do, though, is gather everyone together," I said as if I hadn't heard her speak. "We're all going back up to the forest, to where the portals are."

"But I can't make the portals work," she said, half a wail.

"I know," I assured her. "I have some thoughts on that. But the first thing we have to do is get everyone away from this house. If you lead them back to the forest glade, will they follow you?"

Gladys balled her hands into fists, fighting some internal battle. But in the end she slumped in defeat and gave me a reluctant nod.

"Do you think that will break the spell?" Kara asked me in a whisper.

"It's maybe in the category of 'can't hurt to try'?" Tlalli speculated.

"I think I know how to break the spell," I said. "I just need everyone a safe distance away first."

"Before you do what?" Kara asked, alarmed.

I didn't answer straight away. But only because I was still gazing at the patterns I saw in the spells around the gingerbread house.

Tlalli seemed to realize what had my attention, and she too turned to look at the weave of spells. Then Kara joined us in gazing at what I'm sure to Thorge and Thorbjorn looked like nothingness.

"Powerful magic," Kara said.

"Delicate spellwork," Tlalli added.

"But very inexpertly maintained," I said. "Do you see it? Well, maybe it looks different to you than to me. But I see bind runes that are falling apart."

"Knots are fraying," Tlalli mumbled in agreement.

"But the power," Kara insisted. "My goodness, it's almost as strong as your grandmother's mead hall."

"My grandmother maintains those spells daily," I said. "Well, you know that. You and I have both helped her with that on various occasions."

"So you think this is what your grandmother's mead hall would look like without maintenance?" Kara asked.

"It would just sit there in Runde, luring people in for an evening of mead and ale, music and song, tales and good company?" Tlalli asked.

"And then wouldn't let them go," I said with a sigh. "I don't know. I think so? But I'm going to leave it to my grandmother to make the call on this one. We're just going to get everyone up the hill first."

"And if your grandmother agrees with you?" Thorbjorn asked.

I looked up at him with a halfhearted grin. "Then I'm afraid she's going to ask you to burn this whole thing to the ground."

"That's going to smell absolutely delicious," Thorge said.

But it was a joke none of us laughed at.

CHAPTER TWENTY-TWO

I'VE NEVER BEEN a video game person, let alone the sort who plays zombie-shooting video games. But I would have to imagine that if anyone wanted to play a really challenging zombie game, it would involve trying to get twelve of them safely up a steep slope and then staying in a group while walking through a dense forest.

I mean, they wanted to follow Gladys, so that part worked fine. But they were clumsy, and they kept sliding down the hill. No matter how many times Thorge or Thorbjorn caught them by the elbow and got them climbing again, as soon as they had one back on their feet, another would start sliding back towards the valley again.

It was probably just as well none of us had any idea how long it was taking. Hunger was gnawing at my belly, and I was so tired it felt like my skull was stuffed with cotton. But I had no concept of what time it would be when we finally made it back to Duluth.

Or when that would even happen. Because once we reached the point in the forest where our tracks all began, there was no sign of the blue light of an open portal anywhere.

Tlalli and I tried every trick we knew to sense magic, crawling around all the trees. There were several that were bent into natural arches by their interlocking boughs, and we were sure those were the places where portals were bound to appear. Only we didn't sense anything magical about any of them.

Kara, for her part, was too worn out to even try to help. Which, given her zeal for pitching in, was saying something. She just sat on the soft, needle-strewn forest floor with her back against an oak tree and dozed. Her hands were resting gently on her belly, but I think that was more for her own comfort than any worry about her baby.

"We should have brought some gingerbread up with us," Tlalli said. So I guess her stomach was growling as fiercely as mine.

"Too likely to be cursed, right?" I said. Not for the first time.

"I wasn't going to eat off the house itself," she grumbled. "But fresh from the oven? That must've been curse-free, right?"

"Gladys, were you buying ingredients out in the big world?" I asked.

She blinked at me in surprise. "No. They're always just there when I need them. Like the stove in the house always has food, and the well always has water."

"Yeah. Cursed gingerbread," I said to Tlalli.

She just shrugged, too tired to argue.

I longed to lean against Thorbjorn, to let the soporific silence of the warm forest around us lull me to sleep. Alas, he and Thorge both had their hands full keeping our rescued victims from wandering back down towards the valley.

Although even as I thought that, I realized that the brothers weren't the only ones herding the house builders now. Karen and Hailey were both helping out. They, at least, were coming out of whatever spell fog had kept them so forgetful and compliant.

Maybe there really was still hope for the others.

"Honestly, I don't even know which of these I came through in the first place anymore," Tlalli grumbled, finally giving up the search for a magical trigger that I had stopped looking for some time before. "I wish I'd remembered I had chalk in my pocket before I left this grove. I felt like I had everything memorized at the time when I went searching for food, but clearly I didn't."

"It's this place," I assured her. "I just wish we hadn't lost track of Mjolner."

"He got you close enough to find me," Tlalli said. "Maybe he assumed you could take it from there. Because, you know, you did."

"Sure, but where did he go that was more important than being with me?"

That totally wasn't a complaint, although even I could hear the edge of a whine in my tired voice. No, it was an actual question.

Where *did* he have to go?

And then, as if in answer, I heard a meow.

We all whipped our heads around, even Kara, fully awake now, as we hunted for any sign of my cat.

He meowed again. And then he stepped into view, out of an arch made of twisted trees that was several feet away from where we all were. A spot neither Tlalli nor I had checked for magic.

As happy as I was to see him again, and the blue light of a portal remaining pleasantly open behind him, I was downright ecstatic when who should appear in the forest grove behind him but my grandmother. She had the cranky look of someone up before their bedtime, but was dressed in her usual jeans, flannel shirt and hiking boots with a walking stick in one hand.

And the unmistakable shape of a picnic basket in the other.

Before I could even react to that, Tlalli cried out, "Saoirse!" A tall woman with her red and gray hair twisted in a truly elaborate array of braids stepped out of the portal to stand beside my grandmother. She was dressed in black jeans, practical black leather boots that were not quite combat boots, and a gorgeous emerald green tunic-length sweater knit in a complex array of Celtic knotwork. And she had a picnic basket in each hand.

"I've never been happier to see you, Mormor," I said even as I reached for that basket.

But she pulled it away from my grasp. "This one is for the others." Then she looked around until she saw where Hailey was desperately trying to keep all three of the teenagers from pushing past her to go back the way we'd come, back to the gingerbread house. My grandmother gripped the basket a little tighter, then marched through the trees to grab young Mark by the elbow.

"Here, boy," she said, shoving the basket into Hailey's arms so she could dig into it. Then she came out with a phial of something an unnaturally bright shade of green. Like chartreuse, only brighter. "Drink this, and I'll give you a waffle."

She couldn't have sounded *less* grandmotherly if she had tried. But Mark was pretty pliable. When she shoved the phial into his hands, he took it. And when she guided it up to his lips, he drank it down.

I could see life coming back to his eyes even before he took the waffle she was holding out for him.

"What's in that?" Hailey asked, peering down into the basket she was holding.

"Magic," my grandmother said simply, then pulled out another phial before closing in on Kimberly.

"I have more conventional food," Saoirse said, setting her own baskets on the ground beside where Kara was sitting. "Ham, cheese and tomato sandwiches on homemade black bread. You can thank my coven; they love throwing food together. Although your cat," she added just to me with a piercing gaze, "was scarcely patient about the scant few minutes we made him wait while we packed the baskets."

Mjolner gave an indignant meow, not at all sorry for whatever behavior he had exhibited. While in Northern Ireland, apparently.

"We really appreciate it," I said. "And that you're here at all. I gather Mjolner fetched you?"

"I do believe he went to Nora first, but it was lovely to be includ-ed," Saoirse said. Although the way she said "lovely" made it sound like she really meant anything but.

"Er," I said.

"Duluth is more your domain than Nora's," Tlalli said, playing the role of peacekeeper even as she helped herself to two of the sand-wiches in the basket. Well, she had been trapped here the longest, and I doubted the crushed protein bar I had given her had done more than taken the edge off her hunger.

Mjolner meowed again, sounding self-satisfied.

"It's worse than we feared," my grandmother said as she came over to stand by Saoirse's side.

"What do you mean?" I asked.

"I knew when I saw the portal in the trees that Mjolner led me to that there would be time slippage here," my grandmother said as she fished one of the sandwiches out of the basket. She broke it in two, handed one of the halves to Saoirse, and took a bite before going on. "This is more Saoirse's expertise than mine. Fairy magic."

"There are no fairies here," Saoirse said.

"No, not anymore. It's been fairy-abandoned for quite some time. The land is quite depleted. And yet the magic remains," my grandmother said, gesturing to the portals as she took another bite from her sandwich.

She had been doing something, some powerful magic that had left her drained. Aside from the hearty appetite she was displaying, I could see the circles under her eyes now that she was standing closer to me.

"There's magic in a gingerbread house the size of a palace nearby that you're going to want to take a closer look at when you have a minute," I told them both. But I still didn't quite understand what they were telling me. "You're saying it's fairy magic that affects time and memory? But you fixed Mark and the other kids. Are the adults too far gone?"

"I've given out everything I brought with me," my grandmother said. "I can cook up more batches back home, enough to get them all well again. But it's going to take some time."

"Well, we didn't really think we'd get everyone back home *today*," Saoirse said.

"How long have we been gone?" I asked. "Because the two of you are talking like you spent days preparing for your trip here."

"Well, days? Yes and no," Saoirse said, making a waffling gesture with her hand.

"When you follow Mjolner back through the portal you came in from, you'll find about an hour has passed," my grandmother said.

"And the others? How much time has passed for them? I mean, if everyone came in through a different portal..." I just trailed off, not entirely sure exactly what I meant, or what I was asking.

But my grandmother understood what I was only half articulating. "The three kids came together," she said, pointing at David, Mark and Kimberly. "We can give it a few more minutes for the tonic and what I put in the waffle batter to take full effect, but then they can go right back home again. Like with you, it will only be an hour or so since they left. Not even Mjolner can pinpoint it closer than that."

"And the others?" I asked.

"Like I said, we're going to give it a minute. They might remember where they came from, in which case Mjolner can also guide them home, within an hour of when they left it."

"But if they don't remember?"

"Then they'll be coming home with me," my grandmother said. She looked at Saoirse, who first shrugged and then nodded. "Yes, they'll stay in the hamlet outside of Villmark. Signi can help keep them all calm. When they realize what's been happening, there might be some feelings of panic. But once all their memories are restored and they're ready to go, Mjolner can take everyone back."

"Everyone?" Tlalli said, looking over to where Gladys was sitting alone, apart from everyone, picking at a waffle that my grandmother must have given her.

"Well, I gave her the same medicines as the others, but frankly, I don't think they're ever going to work for her," my grandmother said softly.

"Because she hasn't forgotten as much as the others?" I asked. "Or because she was the only one who was coming and going?"

"She's the one who's actually fairy-kissed," Saoirse said. "That's not fixable. She'll just have to carry on just as she is with what memories she has."

"Forever?" Tlalli asked.

At first, I thought she was holding out hope that Gladys could remember where she came from. That Mjolner could lead her, too, back to her baby brother. Not that she could sit by the fire and rock his cradle even if she did. She wasn't his big sister anymore. But maybe she could be his nanny or something?

Only that wasn't what Tlalli meant. And I uttered a single, "Oh," when it sunk in.

"What?" Kara asked, looking from me to Tlalli and back again.

"Fairy-kissed," Tlalli said. "No one knows if that actually means immortal. But no one who has been fairy-kissed has ever been known to die. So, probably?"

"What does that mean? For her?" Kara asked.

"For now, it means she stays with Signi," my grandmother said. "Maybe someday she'll find a new home of her own. But for now, it's too likely that on her own she'd just stumble into another magical mess she doesn't have the skills or knowledge to get herself out of."

"So she is a witch with no community, like you said before?" I asked.

But my grandmother shook her head sadly. "No, she's not a witch. She was just a normal human girl."

"Who crossed paths with a fairy, one with power and a will to use that power for mischief," Saoirse said. "I know the type. I might even know the fairy. I'll definitely have some questions for Gladys. But later, when we're not so busy."

"Gladys will be cared for," my grandmother assured me. "At the same time, we'll be taking care that she does no more harm to others. Either deliberately or not."

"So if everyone is eventually going to go home again, save Gladys, and everyone will be returned almost to the moment that they left, everything is okay then?" I asked.

"Not entirely," Kara said with a frown. At my questioning look, she went on. "The ones that look like they were kids when they came here but outgrew their clothes? Even if we just put them back, so much time has passed. They can't pick up their lives again."

"No, those will have different choices to make," my grandmother said. "Once their memories return, and probably after a lot of talks with Signi about everything they've been through, they'll be able to decide what comes next for them. They can return to where they came from, or they can stay with us."

"I imagine they'll choose to stay," Saoirse said. "The magic worked the way it did for them because they're from the most distant past, and from more distant places as well. If you had to choose between the modern world and the Dark Ages, when no one in the Dark Ages even recognizes you as family anymore, which would you pick?"

I dodged that question entirely, my mind preoccupied with something else. "So everyone who was taken from Duluth itself, they're the more recent ones? They'll be going back right where they left?"

"Certainly," my grandmother said, then added, "Give or take an hour."

"But that explains why there was no history of missing persons," Tlalli said, quickly picking up on my thread. "Because they were never missing. Because we're about to put them back."

"Well, there is a tiny exception to that," my grandmother said with a wince of sympathy.

"Karen and Hailey," I guessed.

"Yes. Because they were tied up with the three of you and your own magic, they'll have to come back out with you."

"An hour from when we left," Kara said.

"Exactly. People are going to remember they were gone, but they'll be back, safe and sound," my grandmother said. "It's as happy an ending as we could manage."

She shot Saoirse a glance, and Saoirse nodded curtly.

But there was something about that gesture that made me wonder again just how long they had been planning our rescue. With Saoirse's fairy barrow on top of our own fairy forest magic both messing with the flow of time, there was no way I was ever doing that math.

One thing I did know, it hadn't been easy. It had taken them time to figure out what to do, and time to make all the preparations.

Just what was in that liqueur and those waffles? The sort of magic spell that has steps over every cycle of the moon? For, like, months and months?

Then Mjolner meowed, drawing everyone's attention.

It was time to start getting people home.

CHAPTER TWENTY-THREE

THERE WAS a lot of work to be done, and a lot of time passed while we did it. But because that time was as much inside the fairy forest as in Duluth, I completely lost track of the hours, days… frankly, it could've even been weeks.

But when it was all done, every person who had been lured into the fairy forest by Gladys—willingly or not—and who had regained their memories was back where they belonged. I have no idea how Mjolner navigated the space and time involved, but it seemed to work. In ones and twos, everyone followed him through the arches under the trees and vanished. Then Mjolner came back to do the same thing all over again with the next batch.

I had been worried at first about how old most of the victims were. But aside from the few in the tattered remains of very small clothing, most of them had been more like Karen than like the ones who had come through as naïve children.

They had been adults who had seen Gladys, older and not quite acting right, and had offered their help.

When Saoirse explained to me how their memories in the fairy forest were going to fade—and quickly—when they returned to their normal lives, I was actually kind of happy about that. No one should remember how badly being a Good Samaritan had hurt them. They didn't deserve that.

Hailey and Karen remembered, though. They had sworn they would never speak of it, and aside from the fact that even if they wanted to, where would they find anyone who believed them, I took them at their word. They both knew that the magic portal in the alley was something that was no longer a danger to anyone.

But that was only because of the other half of the work we had been doing. Because after we had gotten everyone that Gladys had ever abducted either back home with their families or safely tucked away in the hamlet north of Villmark until they were ready for their next steps, that's when the real work began.

Which started just as I knew it would, with Thorbjorn and Thorge searching the interior of that gingerbread palace thoroughly to be sure we'd left no one with the brain capacity of a zombie behind—we hadn't—before burning the palace to the ground.

Thorge said it smelled just as amazing as he'd hoped. But I wasn't there, so I don't know. I think maybe he was only saying that to make Kara smile.

But, I mean, I know they weren't chopping down trees to use for fuel because Saoirse nixed that idea in a heartbeat. Burning anything in a fairy forest is a big no-no, I guess. Even in the parts where the magic had been depleted and it was essentially just a misplaced chunk of the Black Forest from the Dark Ages.

Which meant they'd had to use some kind of accelerant to burn that palace down. And while I just know that probably smelled pretty strongly of something, that something was the farthest thing from delicious.

Meanwhile, those of us with magic were busy inside the forest grove itself. Because everything down in the valley was some offshoot this particular fairy had created solely for the purpose of making mischief, and it had to go. The magic that pulled those places here had to be undone, and those places returned to where they were meant to be. Nothing was going to remain save the cluster of portals wrapped inside living trees, and the scant bit of old-growth forest that surrounded it.

My grandmother insisted that letting go of that extra magical space was easier than reeling it in had been in the first place. I'm quite willing to take her word for that. After helping retract that particular pocket dimension back to its proper size, there was no way I ever wanted to mess with that level of magic ever again.

I mean, we expended a lot of magic. A *lot*. Like, way more than the spells I helped my grandmother weave that protected her mead hall. And that had been a lot of high-level magic.

Granted, my grandmother and Saoirse together did the bulk of the work. But Tlalli and I helped all we could. Mostly that was support work, but the support work was feeding our mentors with all the raw power our relative youth could summon so they could craft with it.

We were both drained. And I knew that Kara desperately wanted to contribute, but that wasn't possible. She didn't complain, and I could see every time she felt another stab of feeling about being side-lined emerge that she redirected her thoughts to the baby that was on the way. It was hard for her. But it was a good thing that Thorge was there with nothing else to do but be there for her. Because I was far too tired to be of any use as a source of comfort.

But when we were done, not only did we have a self-contained little forest grove accessible to anyone who could see the portal in the alley in Duluth, we also had a second portal on the far side of that grove that also always stood open, ready for use.

And that portal led to the spot just outside of Villmark where Mjolner had brought my grandmother.

That's right. We had a permanent shortcut from Villmark to Duluth.

Well, there was a bit of a walk from Villmark proper to the arched trees deep in the woods. It would take the better part of a morning for anyone to get there.

But the point was, Kara's mother and sister and anyone else who wanted to visit the expectant couple could do it on their own. No Ingrid and her trusty Volkswagen necessary.

It was pretty nice.

Once it was all set up, Mjolner went to fetch Kara's parents and sister, and together with Tlalli, Jesús, and Jesús' new girlfriend Olive—who was very cool and made a great first impression on all of us—we all sat down for dinner. It was very cramped inside that small apartment, but Michael and Karen next door had offered their own kitchen as an offsite staging area, which Kara was happy to make use of.

As tired as I was when all the company had finally gone home again and Thorbjorn and I had finished helping Kara and Thorge with the mountain of dishes left behind, I didn't want to spend even one more night sleeping on their living room floor. I wanted to be home again, back in my own magnificent bed in my own majestic bedroom with its glorious views of Villmark itself, framed by the autumn-colored hills of northern Minnesota.

Alas, for me, that didn't mean a quick trip through a couple of fairy portals and then a walk through the forest back home. Because I still had my car here, in Duluth. Thorbjorn and I were going to have to drive it back home one last time.

It was only when I was unlocking the passenger door for Thorbjorn that I looked up and saw the moon emerging over the buildings to the east of where we were standing.

It was the night of the full moon. With all the time slippage, I thought I had missed it. I was glad I hadn't.

It was a supermoon, and very well named. It looked so close, like I could reach out and touch it. It beamed down at me in all of its silvery glory, and I just felt completely at peace.

"What is it?" Thorbjorn asked me, apparently not able to read the sudden new expression on my face.

"Nothing," I said, then circled around the car to get into the driver's side.

He ducked into the passenger seat and went through all the necessary steps of getting his oversized frame situated in my snug little car. Then he waited as I started the engine, checked all my mirrors, and backed out onto the road and headed uphill.

But once I had pulled out onto the highway that would take us the rest of the way home, he said, "It isn't nothing. You looked like you were in awe of the moon."

"The moon is awesome," I said, gesturing to where we could see it, throwing its silver light all over the surface of Lake Superior.

"It is," he agreed. "Perhaps I should say, you looked like you'd never seen it before. Like you were gobsmacked."

"Well, it's extra huge," I said. "But no, you're right. I just felt something when I was looking up at it."

"What did you feel?"

"Like everything was going to be okay," I said. "With Gladys and all the people she abducted for sure. Kara and the baby, them too. Us. Loke."

"The moon told you all that," he said.

"No, I just felt it. In my bones. Everything is going to be fine in the end."

"Hm," Thorbjorn said, but his attention wasn't on the moon, which I was still stealing as many glances at as driving the car down the highway would allow me.

No, he was alternatively looking at my phone mounted on the dashboard then off to the west.

Everything to the west was dark. No sign of the sun, now long since set, but also no sign of stars or anything else.

"A storm is blowing in," he said. "I smell snow."

"You do," I said, my tone only somewhat skeptical. "Or maybe you saw something on the weather app on my phone that tipped you off?"

"It's your fault for showing me how it works," he said.

Between the road ahead of us and the moon off to my right, I sneaked a look at the screen of my phone. There was indeed a weather advisory in my notifications. Snow expected. Perhaps as much as a foot. And blowing winds, and an Arctic chill.

"This early in the season, it will surely melt again in a few days," I said.

"You are quite determined to be optimistic, aren't you?" Thorbjorn said, amused.

"Well, maybe?" I said. "Mostly I'm just thinking, I can just get us home in time if I put my foot down on the gas a little. Then, by the time the snow starts, we'll be snuggled up under warm blankets, maybe with a fire going. A cat curled up between us if he's in the mood. Then I can just nap and rest up while the storm blows outside, keeping trouble at bay for a few days, anyway. I don't know. Could be cozy."

"I would enjoy a little coziness," Thorbjorn said, his tone far too grave for the actual words coming out of his mouth. But that was okay.

Sometimes that was the way to do it. You had to be just as serious and driven about the cozy things that recharged you as about the responsibilities you could never set aside.

And sure, the snow might be early, but we were overdue for the coziness.

I pressed down on the gas to urge my Volkswagen along just a little bit faster. The little car shook from the acceleration, but I wasn't worried. I knew we'd make it home in time.

The moonlight bathing over the hood of my car told me so. Because Thorbjorn and I had earned a little quiet moment.

And we were going to make the most of it.

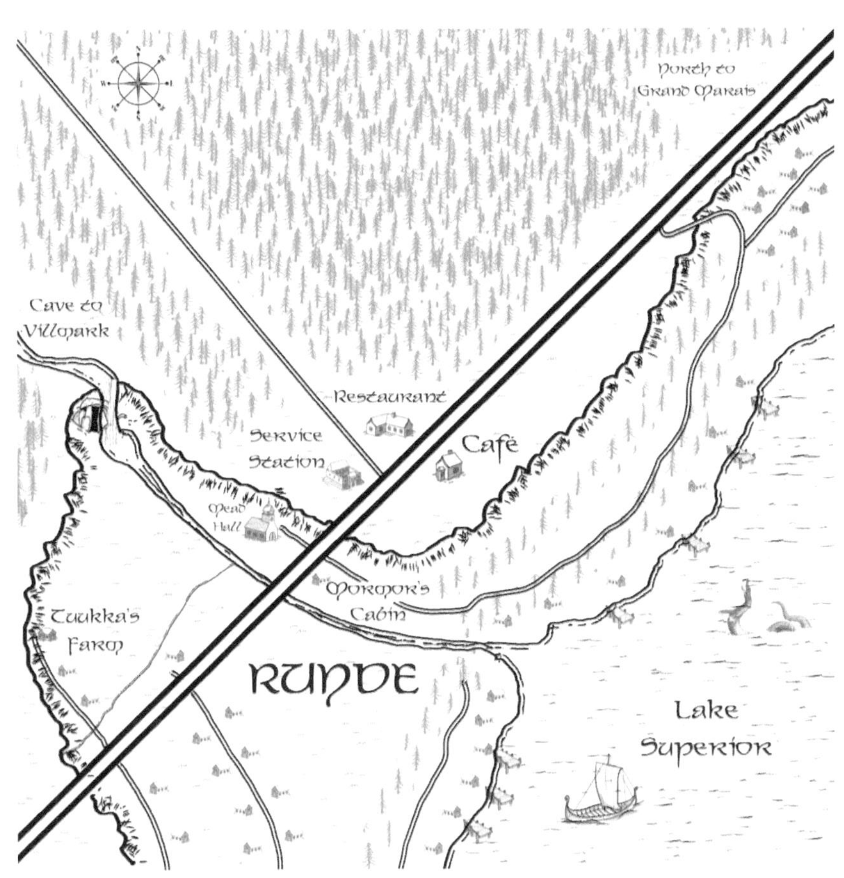

North to
Grand Marais
Cave to
Villmark
Restaurant
Service
Station
Café
Mead
Hall
Mormor's
Cabin
Tuukka's
Farm
RUNDE
Lake
Superior

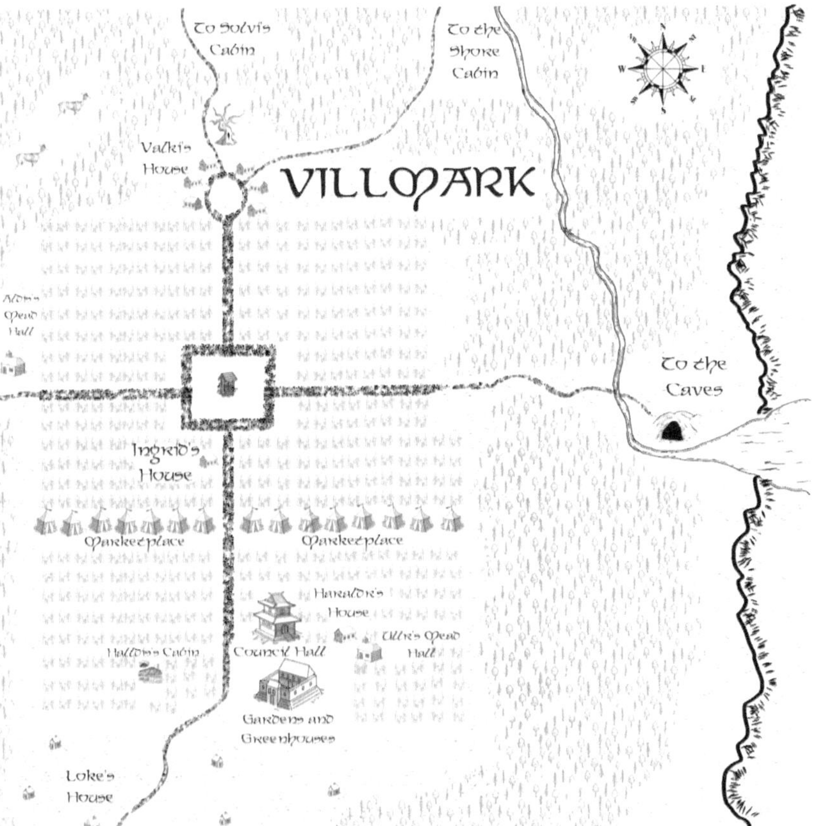

To Solvi's Cabin
To the Shore Cabin
Valki's House
VILLMARK
Aldis's Mead Hall
To the Caves
Ingrid's House
Marketplace
Marketplace
Harald's House
Halldr's Cabin
Council Hall
Ullr's Mead Hall
Gardens and Greenhouses
Loke's House

CHECK OUT BOOK SIXTEEN!

The Viking Witch will return in Ashes Beneath the Tree, out July 14, 2026 direct from me or August 11, 2026 in stores everywhere. Available for preorder now!

Ingrid Torfudottir moved to the North Shore of Lake Superior intending to live with her grandmother while pursuing a career as a book illustrator. Instead, she discovered her true calling as a volva—a Viking witch—serving a village founded in the Viking age by Norse settlers escaping some terrible enemy whose identity was lost to time.

Now she lives in the hidden town of Villmark, protected by magic from the perceptions of anyone in the larger world. But more lands lie beyond Villmark. Lands that extend through places where time moves at different speeds. Lands filled with trolls, giants, and witches lurking in magical towers. Lands, in short, where the older magics still thrive.

Such places exist outside of Ingrid's domain as volva under normal circumstances. But when Ingrid's ward Esja gets tangled up with a young man with a dark history, one who lures her out into those wilder lands, what happens next is far from normal circumstances.

Someone wants that young man dead. Someone immensely powerful. But not as powerful as those who ride during these, the longest, darkest nights of the year. The ones that no human can control. Just to see them is to see your own doom.

But if your foe wields the old magics, sometimes calling on the oldest magic of all is your only hope.

The Viking Witch will return in Ashes Beneath the Tree, out July 14, 2026 direct from me or August 11, 2026 in stores everywhere. Available for preorder now!

THE WITCHES THREE
COZY MYSTERIES

In case you missed it, check out **Charm School**, the first book in the complete **Witches Three Cozy Mystery Series**!

Amanda Clarke thinks of herself as perfectly ordinary in every way. Just a small-town girl who serves breakfast all day in a little diner nestled next to the highway, nothing but dairy farms for miles around. She fits in there.

But then an old woman she never met dies, and Amanda was named in her will. Now Amanda packs a bag and heads to the big city, to Miss Zenobia Weekes' Charm School for Exceptional Young Ladies. And it's not in just any neighborhood. No, she finds herself on Summit Avenue in St. Paul, a street lined with gorgeous old houses, the former homes of lumber barons, railroad millionaires, even the writer F. Scott Fitzgerald. Why, Amanda can practically hear the jazz music still playing across the decades.

Scratch that. The music really, literally, still plays in the backyard of the charm school. Because the house stretches across time itself. Without a witch to protect this tear in the fabric of the world, anything can spill over. Like music.

Or like murder.

Charm School, the first book in the complete **Witches Three Cozy Mystery Series!**

THE WEAL & WOE BOOKSHOP
WITCH MYSTERIES

In case you missed it, check out **The Teashop Terror**, the first book in the complete **Weal & Woe Bookshop Witch Mystery Series**!

No one knows more about every branch of magic than Tabitha Greene. She devoted years to studying the most esoteric texts, hunting down the most obscure source materials, and deciphering the most cryptic ancient scrolls. But her career in academia hits a dead end when no wizard will take her on as an apprentice.

Just because, despite being descended from two long and prestigious lines of witches, her attempts to actually perform any magic always fail. Often spectacularly.

But no more college means no more dorm life. And no magical skills means no real job skills, at least, not in the witchy world. And a life spent moving from school to school every few months was a life without real friendships. She finds herself alone with nowhere to go.

Then an uncle she barely remembers offers her a summer job, running his bookstore over the summer. The Weal and Woe Bookstore, located in a magical pocket world within a block of buildings just north of the old Mill District of Minneapolis, Minnesota.

Not exactly the pinnacle of all her hopes and dreams. But it's just for one summer, right?

Or so Tabitha tells herself. But unbeknownst to her, the Weal and Woe Bookstore is about to change her life.

The Teashop Terror, the first book in the complete **Weal & Woe Bookshop Witch Mystery Series**!

The Ritchie and Fitz Sci-Fi Murder Mysteries starts with **Murder on the Intergalactic Railway**.

For Murdina Ritchie, acceptance at the Oymyakon Foreign Service Academy means one last chance at her dream of becoming a diplomat for the Union of Free Worlds. For Shackleton Fitz IV, it represents his last chance not to fail out of military service entirely.

Strange that fate should throw them together now, among the last group of students admitted after the start of the semester. They had once shared the strongest of friendships. But that all ended a long time ago.

But when an insufferable but politically important woman turns up murdered, the two agree to put their differences aside and work together to solve the case.

Because the murderer might strike again. But more importantly, solving a murder would just have to impress the dour colonel who clearly thinks neither of them belong at his academy.

Murder on the Intergalactic Railway, the first book in **The Ritchie**

and Fitz Sci-Fi Murder Mysteries, available everywhere books are sold.

FREE EBOOK!

Like exclusive, free content?

If you'd like to receive "A Collection of Witchy Prequels", a free collection of short story prequels to the Witches Three Cozy Mystery and Viking Witch Mystery series, as well as other free stories throughout the year, go to my website CateMartin.com to subscribe to my newsletter! This eBook is exclusively for newsletter subscribers and will never be sold in stores. Check it out!

ABOUT THE AUTHOR

Cate Martin has written stories which have appeared in **Mystery, Crime and Mayhem** quarterly magazine as well as in the annual **Holiday Spectacular** Advent calendar of Christmas stories. She is also the author of three witch mystery series: **The Witches Three Cozy Mysteries**, and **The Viking Witch Mysteries** and **The Weal and Woe Bookshop Witch Mysteries**. She currently lives in Minneapolis, Minnesota. You can learn more about her work at CateMartin.com.

Ashes Beneath the Tree (available July 14, 2026 direct from me or August 11, 2026 in stores everywhere)

The Viking Witch Mysteries Books 1-3

The Viking Witch Mysteries Books 4-6

The Viking Witch Mysteries Books 7-9

The Weal & Woe Bookshop Witch Mystery Series

The Teashop Terror

The Salon & Spa Scandal

The Bookseller Blunder

The Entrepreneur Enigma

The Novelty Shop Nightmare

The Courtyard Conundrum

Short Story Collections

Bubbly, Bicycles and Brides

The Dorothy Lundegaard Mysteries

Fruitcake, Festivities and Firelight